25p

The Hardy Boys®
in
The Clue in the

D0714346

This Armada book belongs to:

_____

_____

_____

Other Hardy Boys® Mystery Stories in Armada

The Hardy Boys® Mystery Stories

The Clue
in the Embers

Franklin W. Dixon

Armada

First published in the U.K. in 1972 by
William Collins Sons & Co. Ltd., London and Glasgow.
First published in Armada in 1975 by
Fontana Paperbacks,
8 Grafton Street, London W1X 3LA.

This impression 1984.

Printed in Great Britain by
William Collins Sons & Co. Ltd., Glasgow

CONTENTS

Frank crashed into the man, sending him sprawling.

·1· *A Strange Inheritance*

THE shrill ringing of the Hardy telephone greeted Frank and Joe as they swung into the driveway after a midsummer ball practice at the Bayport High playing fields.

"Hurry!" Mrs Hardy called a moment later. "It's the third time Tony Prito has phoned this morning!"

"Must be an important message," said blond, seventeen-year-old Joe to his brother Frank, dark-haired and a year older. "Be right there, Mom!"

Clearing the porch steps in two strides, Joe hurried in to the phone. "Hello, Tony. What's up?"

Tony's voice was serious. "How would you and Frank like to see some shrunken heads?"

"See *what!*" Joe gasped.

"Six shrunken human heads!"

"Where are they?"

Tony replied excitedly, "I've inherited a lot of mysterious curios from my uncle Roberto. He had a shop full of them in New York when he died. The shipment, including the shrunken heads, will arrive at the Bayport station at one-twenty."

"Wait till I tell Frank!" Joe exclaimed, and promised that the Hardys would be at the Prito house by one o'clock. "We'll help you load the crates."

"I may need you fellows for more than loading

crates," Tony remarked, his voice grave again. "Tell you when you get here."

Joe hurried outside and relayed to Frank the story of the strange shipment. His brother's eyebrows lifted. "No wonder Tony phoned three times," Frank observed as he followed his brother into the house. "This sounds as though we might have run smack into another mystery."

"Time for lunch!" Mrs Hardy told them as they walked into the kitchen. Then the slender, attractive woman asked, "What's this about a mystery?" The boys told her briefly what Tony had said.

Mrs Hardy smiled. "You're both just like your dad."

Fenton Hardy, the boys' father, an internationally famous detective, had served many years with the New York City police force. Later, he had settled in Bayport, a bustling seaport of fifty thousand inhabitants. From his big stone house at the corner of Elm and High streets he carried on a highly successful career as a private investigator, but he liked nothing better than working with his two sons, solving mysteries.

"Shall we call Chet and ask him to come along to help carry crates?" Joe asked. "He needs the exercise."

Chet Morton was the Hardys' chubby pal who often went along with them to follow up clues. He lived on a farm about a mile from Bayport.

Frank shook his head. "Better not take the time. If Tony's as worried as he seems to be, we'd better eat and get over there as quickly as possible. It's almost one o'clock now."

Within ten minutes the boys were on their way to Tony's house. They found their friend sitting on the front steps. One of the Prito Construction Company's large trucks was parked at the kerb. Tony wore an anxious look as he waved to the Hardys.

"What's this all about?" Frank asked, as they hurried up the path.

Tony's expression relaxed a little. "Some inheritance, eh?" he said. "All kinds of weird stories connected with the curios. But I'm puzzled why anyone would want to buy the collection without examining it to see what it's worth."

"What!" Joe exclaimed.

Reaching into his sports shirt pocket, Tony pulled out a telegram and showed it to the boys.

Signed with the single name *Valez*, the message was an offer to buy unseen, for two hundred dollars, the entire collection of curios.

"This arrived yesterday," Tony explained. "And you notice that Valez, whoever he is, says he's going to phone this afternoon and make arrangements for picking up the stuff."

Suspicious, the Hardys glanced at each other. The man certainly was not giving Tony much time to consider the offer. Frank suggested at once that the collection might be worth much more than two hundred dollars.

"Sure," said Joe. "I wouldn't take his offer."

"Right," Frank continued. "Valez is too eager to make a deal. And he doesn't present even one credential. Besides, I think he has a nerve to assume you're going to sell him the curios before you've had a chance to have them valued."

"Do you have a list of all the curios, Tony?" Joe asked.

"No, not a complete one," Tony replied, "but this letter from the estate's executor, a bank in New York City, mentions some of the items." From a pocket he removed a long, folded envelope. The boys scanned the paragraph that told of the curios.

"Look!" Joe exclaimed. "You even have some Moorish scimitars!"

"What about them?" Tony asked.

Frank, who had done some research in connection with a case, explained that a scimitar is a crescent-shaped sabre used originally by Moorish horsemen, and as late as the Wars of Napoleon. Made of fine Damascus steel, often with guards of gold set with precious stones, these antique weapons are rare and valuable.

"And here!" Frank continued. "The letter mentions the South American shrunken heads you told Joe about on the phone!"

These heads, or *tsanstas*, the letter explained, in spite of laws against their sale or barter in both Peru and Ecuador, have a considerable value in the souvenir market.

The savage Andean Indians used to take the heads of their enemies in local warfare. After the removal of the skull from the severed head, the rest was reduced by boiling to the size of a man's fist. The eyes and lips were pinned and laced, and the interior treated with hot stones and sand. With the use of a local herb, the hair remained long and kept its original lustre.

"Pretty barbaric," Tony remarked.

"I don't suppose these heads are as valuable as many of the other objects," Frank said. "But you shouldn't sell a single item until you've had a chance to find out the value of the collection."

Tony agreed.

"We'd better get started for the station," Joe urged. "The train's just about due."

Tony slipped the telegram back into his pocket along with the letter. The trio started off.

Brr-r-r-ing! The phone in the Prito hallway rang shrilly.

"Maybe it's Valez!" Tony exclaimed.

The Hardys followed their friend into the hallway and Tony picked up the phone. As he listened, his jaw tightened. For several seconds the three boys stood still while the high-pitched voice on the line chattered without a break. Tony nodded to indicate that the caller was Valez.

"No!" Tony said abruptly. "Thank you just the same."

Valez's voice grew louder and angry. Then it stopped.

"I'm sorry," Tony said firmly. "I can't accept your offer."

The Hardys heard Valez snap one more remark at Tony. An awkward silence followed. Then Tony hung up.

"What did he say?" the Hardys asked eagerly.

"Valez threatened me," Tony replied. "He said, 'You'll be sorry for this.' And he's right here in Bayport!"

"Wow!" Joe exploded. "We'd better get down to the station. Valez might try to pull a fast one."

"I'm sure glad that you fellows are along," Tony said nervously, as the trio dashed out of the house.

The train was not yet in sight when the boys arrived at the station. The usual small crowd of idlers and station employees bustled about or stared up the track to watch for the incoming freight train.

Glancing quickly round the platform, the boys saw no one who resembled what they thought Valez might look like. Most of the faces were familiar and the others were those of teenagers.

"Here she comes!" a youngster cried, as the whistle blew before it roared into the station area and ground to a stop.

The boys' hearts beat excitedly in anticipation as they watched the freight agent run his cart to a box-car. The door opened. Crates and cartons were quickly lifted out.

Joe whistled loudly. "Wow! Some haul, Tony!" he exclaimed as box after box, some with strange foreign-looking markings, was piled high on to the cart. The boys watched alertly out of the corner of their eyes for any unusual action or the sudden appearance of any particularly interested persons.

"Okay, Tony!" the agent said, and handed him the bill of lading to be signed.

Without losing a moment, the three boys pulled the cart to the truck and started loading the cases on to it. Working feverishly to finish the job so that they could get home and examine the curios, the boys were glad to have the help of two acquaintances from the platform crowd.

As Joe lifted the last case on to the truck, he said quietly, "Frank, you sit up front with Tony. I'd better stay back here as lookout."

"Okay," his brother agreed and jumped into the cab. Tony climbed to the driver's seat and started the engine.

Sitting atop one of the cases in the open back of the truck, Joe commanded a good view of the station and the public square. "Still no sign of action from Valez," he thought. "I wonder if the whole business was just a hoax."

As they turned into the tree-lined avenue two blocks from Tony's house, Frank slid back the glass in the rear of the cab and said, "This job turned out to be a lot easier than I expected."

Joe was just about to answer when his eye caught sight of an arrowhead-like missile streaking through the air directly towards him!

•2• *A Stolen Curio*

SEEING the missile whizzing towards him, Joe ducked, but he felt a stinging blow on his right arm, which he had flung up to protect himself.

"Stop the truck!" Joe yelled to Tony. "Get that fellow!" He pointed to a man who had dodged from behind a tree and was running away from them at top speed.

The air brakes gripped and the vehicle lurched to a halt. The cab door was flung open by Frank, who raced towards a wooded stretch beyond the sidewalk.

"That fellow has a blowgun!" he called. Frank pursued the assailant into woods at the back of the houses and disappeared.

Meanwhile, Tony eased the truck to the edge of the road. Leaving the engine idling, he slid back the window behind him to see what had happened to Joe.

"Something hit you?" he asked.

"Yes, Tony." Joe showed him a small arrowhead. A tiny paper had been glued to the base of it. Without examining either the arrowhead or the paper, Joe thrust them into a trouser pocket. Asking Tony to guard the truck, he too dashed off in search of his assailant.

Joe sprinted a hundred yards into the woods. Struggling through a stretch of thicket, he called, "Frank! Where are you?"

"Over here!" Frank was standing near a wire fence that bounded two closely spaced factories.

"The blowgun guy jumped the fence," Frank panted, "and ran between the buildings. Never catch him now." Both boys paused to catch their breath.

"We'd better hurry back to the truck," Joe suggested. "This attack might have been just a ruse to get us away from it."

Suddenly they heard the noise of someone crashing through the underbrush towards them. They wondered if it was an accomplice of Joe's attacker, also armed with a blowgun.

"Duck behind this tree!" Frank whispered.

A moment later the figure of Tony Prito appeared in the nearest clearing.

"Tony!" Frank called softly.

Their friend approached the Hardys, a smile of relief on his face. "I just couldn't sit in that truck any longer worrying about you guys. I took the ignition key and lit out after you. Guess I shouldn't have left the truck, though."

The trio ran back towards the street. "Did you get a good look at the man?" Tony asked.

"Not too good," Frank replied. "He's short, thin, dark-complexioned, and has a small moustache."

Joe frowned. "How old do you think he is?"

"I'd say about forty, and a very wiry guy. You should have seen him vault that fence."

To the boys' relief, they found the shipment intact in the truck.

"Joe, you'd better sit up front with us," Tony said. "We can't afford to let that man take another pot shot at you. You might not be so lucky the next time."

Once inside the cab, the boys examined the arrowhead which was made of lead, and the paper which had covered the base of the missile. A message was written on the paper in a scrawled and barely legible script. The pencilled words warned Tony not to dispose of the curios.

"Gosh, what's a fellow supposed to do?" Tony complained. "First Valez threatens me if I don't sell the stuff, and now this guy tells me not to or I'll get in trouble!"

"I'll bet Valez is responsible for both threats," said Joe. "Maybe he has a reason for wanting to confuse you."

"How can we be sure that this warning was fired by Valez?" Frank asked. "There's a good chance that someone else is after the curios, too."

"You mean some enemy of Valez?" Tony asked as he started the truck.

"Possibly," Frank replied.

"At any rate," Joe commented, "we have a full-fledged mystery on our hands."

"You can say that again," Frank agreed.

Tony turned the truck into the driveway of his home and stopped at the rear. He suggested that they carry the cartons and crates of curios into the garage.

"We'll unpack them here," he said, "and carry the articles a few at a time into the house."

By the time they finished, the cases filled the place. The last box to go in was the set of four valuable Damascus steel scimitars.

"Tony," said Frank, "I'm not so sure the garage is

the best place for your curios. Wouldn't they be safer in your cellar?"

"I have an idea," replied Tony. "Why don't I ask the new Howard Museum to take care of them? Maybe I'll give the museum some of them and ask Mr Scath to store the rest for me in return."

"Good idea," said Frank. "I know the stuff will be a lot safer there than in your garage or cellar."

While the Hardys guarded the shipment, Tony went indoors and phoned Mr Scath, the curator.

"Well, now, I don't know quite what to say, Tony," Mr Scath said in reply to the request. "I remember well your uncle Roberto and his shop in New York. He was a delightful and interesting man, and if I remember correctly he was quite absent-minded at times. I liked him very much. But I can't believe that your shipment would include anything of value to our museum."

"But couldn't you at least—?" Tony began.

"I know just what you're going to ask, Tony," Mr Scath interrupted. "Yes. We'll store the curios for you temporarily."

"Swell." Tony explained how urgently he wanted the articles to be protected.

"The museum is open late tonight," said the curator. "I suggest that you bring your curios round about nine o'clock, after closing time. There won't be anybody in the building and I'll have a chance to look at them."

As Tony stepped into the yard he was startled to see a man tiptoeing along the side of the garage and listening. He was short and wore a felt hat pulled low.

Involuntarily Tony yelled. The intruder took off like a streak of lightning. Tony chased the man down the block, but he ran between two houses to another street and escaped in a car.

When Tony told his story to the Hardys, the brothers were worried. "That guy means business!" Joe declared. "We'd better keep a lookout." The boys took turns keeping watch as they inspected the curios.

As time passed, one thing became certain: the collection was worth much more than two hundred dollars.

"Do you realize what time it is?" Frank asked hours later. "Almost six-thirty. Boy, we'd better eat."

"My folks won't be home for dinner," Tony said, "so why don't you call up your house and tell your mother you'll eat here."

"Great idea!" Joe said. "I'll phone."

The boys took their time over the delicious meal and were deep in conversation when suddenly Frank interrupted. "Sh-h!" he warned.

"What's the matter?" Tony asked.

"I heard a noise coming from the garage!"

The boys dashed outside. Seeing that the garage doors were still padlocked, they ran round to the rear. The window was open!

"Careful!" Tony cried, as Joe leaped on to the ledge and climbed in.

Tony opened the lock and entered the garage with Frank. There was no one inside but Joe.

"One of the scimitars is missing!" Frank exclaimed. Only three of the Moorish swords remained in the rack.

Frank and Joe made a frantic search through the neighbourhood but found no trace of the burglar. In disgust they retraced their steps to Tony's house and reported their failure to him.

"Trouble's afoot," said Tony. "Let's wash the dishes and then load the truck before something else happens!"

During the clatter of washing the dishes, the sound

of the doorbell stopped the boys short. Could this be another uninvited visitor?

The tension was broken when Tony opened the door. The caller was the boys' chubby friend, Chet Morton.

"Did I just miss a meal?" Chet chuckled when Frank appeared, still holding a dish towel.

"Yes." Frank laughed. "You missed a meal, but you're just in time to help us load about twenty crates on to Tony's truck."

Chet groaned and slumped into a chair. "Okay," he said. "I walked right into your trap. I'll carry the little ones." Then he added, "But tell me what this is all about."

After giving him a brief resumé, the boys started the job. As darkness began to settle over Bayport, Tony confided to Frank that he thought they should not try to carry out the plan without police protection.

"After what happened today," Frank agreed, "I guess you're right. As a matter of fact, Chief Collig will be at headquarters now. He doesn't go off duty until late in the evening."

Tony phoned and told the chief what had taken place during the day.

"Land sakes, boy," the good-natured officer boomed, "you should've called on us long before now."

Tony estimated that the truck would be loaded by nine-fifteen.

"I'll come out there myself," the chief said. "And I'll bring along a little assistance, even though we shouldn't need it with athletic fellows like you and Chet Morton along!"

With the yard floodlights beamed on them, the four boys worked quickly to have the truck loaded before the arrival of the Bayport police escort.

"Here they come!" Joe called, as Tony swung the last packing case into position.

A squad car, carrying Chief Collig and a patrolman, followed by a motorcycle, pulled up to the kerb. The men waited for the boys to climb on to the truck. Tony switched off the floodlights, ran across the yard, and climbed up behind the wheel. All four boys sat in the big cab.

"Anyone who tries to stop us this time will get a hot reception," Tony remarked as he backed the truck into the street.

With the motorcycle shooting ahead into lead position, and the patrol car in the rear, the convoy started its trek along the dark streets towards the museum.

· 3 · *Fire in the Mummy Case*

THE tree-lined road to the museum, also an approach to the Bayport airfield, ran through one of the loneliest outlying sections of the town. In the long stretches between street lamps, the road was in almost total darkness. The thick foliage of the trees kept the light within a small radius of each pole.

"I'd hate to be walking along here with a blow-gun blower in hiding," Chet said. "It's mighty eerie out this way." He shivered.

At that moment the motorcycle swung to the right and entered the curving, dimly lighted driveway of the ivy-covered museum. As the truck followed, all eyes searched the shrubbery that surrounded the building. But there was no sign of anyone lying in wait.

The massive door of the building creaked open and the slender figure of the curator appeared. Mr Scath hurried down the steps and greeted the boys, then told them to move the crates into the basement.

"Let's step on it!" Tony urged. "The sooner we get this stuff behind that door, the better I'll feel."

As the boys lugged the boxes from the truck, Chief Collig and his men kept an alert watch for Tony's enemies. For fifteen minutes the tense operation continued. Finally, Tony picked up the last crate and called to Chief Collig that the job was finished. After the crate had been placed in the basement, the boys went outside to thank the police official and patrolmen for their help.

The genial chief smiled. "In case you run into any further trouble, call me," he said.

Blinking a signal to the motorcycle officer to follow, he headed back towards town. Mr Scath then bolted the big door, and he and the boys went to the basement to unpack the curios and put them on shelves there.

The curator's eyes flashed with excitement when he finished listing the objects. "I can hardly wait for morning to make a more careful study of these pieces!" he exclaimed. "I can tell you right now I'd like to exhibit these unusual musical instruments with our present collection. Tony, there are some real treasures in this shipment. No wonder some unscrupulous persons are trying to get them."

Tony gulped. "Guess I didn't appreciate what I was getting," he said.

Relieved to know that his inheritance was safe at last

in the museum, Tony assured Mr Scath that he and the Hardys would come over whenever the curator was ready to talk about the curios.

"Of course there will be some items that don't amount to anything," Mr Scath added. "Things like this box, for instance."

For a moment the curator fingered an object that looked like an ordinary cigarette box; it was about four inches long and was made of dark wood. He was just about to toss it into a wastepaper-basket when Frank stopped him.

"If you please, Mr Scath, I'd like to keep this box," he said. "That is, if Tony doesn't want it."

"Help yourself," Tony replied, and Mr Scath handed the object to Frank.

Joe looked at his brother. What did he have in mind? Then Joe recalled one of their father's admonitions: Never throw away any possible evidence where a mystery is concerned.

The curator walked to the storage-room door, and beckoned the boys to precede him. He then locked the door. Frank went ahead, leading the way up the stairs. His footsteps echoed through the main hall. Instinctively he stepped lightly.

"Stop!" Joe whispered suddenly, grabbing his brother's arm from behind. "Did you hear a sound from the other side of the hall?"

"I'm not sure," Frank said softly, gazing towards the room where a mummy and several sarcophagi were on display.

"Listen!" Joe insisted, thrusting his arm out to stop the group. There was no sound.

"Mr Scath," Joe continued in a whisper, "is anybody working in this building?"

"No," the curator assured him. "We're the only ones here."

"Sh-h!" Joe warned.

A sharp scraping noise came from the mummy room. A muffled sound followed.

As Mr Scath switched on all the hall lights, the Hardys, Chet, and Tony ran towards the room where ancient Egyptian treasures were exhibited. Frank stopped at the opening, clicked the switch, and quickly surveyed the pillared room. There was no sign of an intruder among the sarcophagi, one of which held a body three thousand years dead.

"There must be someone in the museum!" Mr Scath whispered nervously. "One of you inspect the balconies upstairs. The rest search this floor!"

Chet Morton, nearest to the spiral steps that led from the main hall to the balconies, gripped the iron rail and started up. But he did not relish the job. Frank and Joe dashed to the left of the Egyptian Room. Mr Scath and Tony headed through the middle of the hall.

"What a spooky place!" Joe exclaimed in hushed tones to his brother, as he looked into an open sarcophagus and saw the painted face of the mummy which lay in an inner coffin made of cedar.

"Don't worry about the spooks!" Frank replied. "I expect to see a blowgun pop out from behind one of those columns!"

Moving stealthily along the outer passage, the brothers reached the other end of the room without catching sight of any intruder. As they headed towards the centre aisle to join the curator, Frank stopped abruptly.

"Do you smell smoke?" he asked, sniffing.

"I sure do," Joe answered, alarmed.

A strong odour of smoke soon filled their nostrils. It was hard to tell where it came from, but both boys dashed among the sarcophagi to locate its source.

"Here it is!" Joe cried out a moment later. "Mr Scath, Frank—come here quick!"

As the curator appeared in the aisle, followed by Frank and Tony, Joe pointed to a slightly opened, ornately designed sarcophagus. Grey-white smoke was pouring from it.

"Give me a hand!" Mr Scath cried. "Lift up the cover!"

The boys got their shoulders against the heavy lid and forced it farther upwards. The smoke thinned into a column, exposing, atop the coffin inside, a cone-shaped pile of embers!

Frank peeled off his polo shirt and smothered the glow that remained in the embers.

"Whoever made this fire must still be in the building!" Mr Scath warned. "No one could get in or out of here without the keys that I have in my pocket. That means someone must have hidden in here before nine o'clock."

"Say!" Joe exclaimed. "Wonder if Chet's found out anything." He called out, but there was no reply from the balcony.

"We'll search the entire building for the intruder," Mr Scath said grimly. "He can't get away. We'll start in the basement."

The Hardys, worried about Chet's failure to answer, decided that one of them should run up to the balcony to check on what might have happened to their friend.

"I'll go," Frank volunteered. "Joe, you help Mr Scath and Tony." Frank headed for the same staircase that Chet had taken.

As the others were about to start for the basement,
Mr Scath decided first to remove the embers from the
sarcophagus. "There's too much danger of their containing a scattered spark or two. Wait here."

The curator got a small shovel and an empty metal
waste-paper basket from his office and returned to the
sarcophagus. He was about to drop the ashes into the
basket when Joe suddenly interrupted.

"Mr Scath, I'd like to take the ashes to our lab to
study them."

"Certainly," the curator agreed. "Mighty good
idea." He had heard of the modern, fully equipped,
crime-detection laboratory that the Hardys had set up
on the first floor of their garage.

Joe got a museum specimen envelope and the curator carefully poured a large sample of the ashes and
charred remains into it. Joe sealed the envelope and
slipped it into his pocket.

"Now let's find the intruder!" Mr Scath urged, and
the trio headed for the basement.

Suddenly, from the balcony, came a crash and a
blood-curdling shriek!

•4• *Skylight Escape*

ELECTRIFIED by the piercing outcry from upstairs, Joe
and Tony dashed up the spiral stairs, with Mr Scath
following as quickly as he could.

Frank had already reached Chet, who admitted
yelling. He said he had not heard Joe calling him before.
"B-but I sure w-wish I had," added Chet, sagging

against the balcony railing opposite the entrance to the American Indian gallery. His face was white and he trembled as he started to explain.

"W-when I got to this spot," he began, "I looked in and saw that figure s-start to move!" He pointed to the tall statue of a Cherokee chieftain that now lay across the passageway.

"How did it get there?" Frank asked.

"It walked, yes, walked, and then it swayed a couple of times before it toppled over," Chet replied.

Mr Scath, reaching the top of the stairs, said, "Calm yourself, Chet. We've had trouble with that figure before. It's off centre. Needs to be balanced."

"B-but what made it walk?" Chet quavered.

The curator's eyes opened wide as a thought struck him. He said the figure could not walk. Probably the intruder had moved it!

"You almost caught him, Chet," Joe remarked.

Chet looked crestfallen at the lost opportunity. Through his being tricked, the stranger had been able to escape. Chet was as indignant now as he had been frightened earlier. "Let's keep looking," he urged, "and find that guy!"

The search for the unknown person continued for half an hour. Methodically the group went from top to bottom of the museum, without finding a trace of the intruder. There were no windows on the ground floor and those on the first were locked.

"How about the skylight?" Frank suggested.

"There's just the one in the prints gallery on the top floor," Mr Scath answered. "I never thought of that. It's not fitted with a special lock!"

Frank went up to the second floor and looked at the skylight. The glass frame was in its properly closed position. But the hasp hung downwards! It was un-locked!

"The intruder went across the roof and down the ivy vines," Frank decided. "A clean getaway!"

The young sleuth returned to the first floor and told Mr Scath of his discovery. The curator explained that the skylight was checked every evening at closing time, so the intruder definitely had hidden in the museum before it closed.

"Boys, we've done all we can. You'd better get some sleep," Mr Scath said. "We can discuss this mystery at another time."

"In the meantime, we may discover something of value about the ashes in this package," Joe added.

After Frank climbed up and locked the skylight, the group headed for the ground floor. Mr Scath asked if Tony would mind following his car in the truck. "With all the odd things going on round here tonight, I don't feel much like driving home alone."

Joe offered to ride with the curator. Tony would follow. The car moved slowly along the drive and turned into the highway.

Its two passengers rode for a couple of blocks in silence. Then Joe remembered the arrowhead that had been fired at him from the blowgun earlier in the day. It was still in his pocket. He brought it out.

"Mr Scath," Joe said, holding the arrowhead in the light from the dashboard, "do you know what country this is from?"

The curator stopped the car and picked up the object from Joe's palm. He looked at it carefully. "Hm-m. It's not North American," Mr Scath said slowly, "and it's not like any I've ever seen before."

"Where would you guess it's from?" Joe prodded.

"That's hard to say," Mr Scath replied. Chuckling, he added, "I wouldn't want to pull a boner in front of a famous young detective."

Joe laughed and slipped the arrowhead back into his pocket. After getting out at Mr Scath's home, Joe stepped up into the truck. Chet was taken home first, then the Hardys.

"See you soon, Tony," Frank called. "Let us know if you hear from Valez again."

The brothers hurried upstairs to their bedroom. Frank stood lost in thought.

Joe eyed him a moment, then remarked, "For a fellow who's been on the go since nine o'clock yesterday morning you don't seem very sleepy." He had noticed that Frank was inspecting the envelope containing the charred remains of the coffin fire.

"I'm not," Frank replied. "Guess I can't sleep until we've made an analysis of these ashes and charred bits. I'm pretty sure it's wood, but I'd like to know what kind."

"Let's try not to wake up Mother," Joe warned. "She'll think we've lost our minds working this late."

The boys removed their shoes, put on moccasins, and headed for their garage laboratory.

"Set up the microtome," Frank suggested. "I'll get the photomicrograph ready."

Joe shook out the contents of the envelope and selected one of the firmer tiny charred pieces. He clamped this in place on the microtome. Then, running a finely honed knife blade delicately through it, Joe cut off a section.

"What thickness?" Joe asked.

"About two thousandths of an inch," Frank replied. Working carefully, Joe cut other tissue-thin sections from several angles, letting them drop on to a glass slide. In a few moments Frank had prepared several photomicrographs of them, showing distinct wood grains.

"Now we'll see what was burning in the sarcophagus," Frank said quietly as he prepared to project the first lantern slide on to the screen in the darkened room.

The enlarged curves in the picture revealed clear patterns. Frank compared them with a chart in an encyclopedia.

"The grain matches the mahogany," he said. The boys examined the pattern again and compared it with further angle shots. "It's Central American mahogany!" Frank concluded.

"Now why would—?" Joe began.

"Just a minute," Frank interrupted thoughtfully. "How about the name Valez?"

"Sounds Spanish enough to have some possible connection," Joe agreed.

"And we know that the missile is not North American," Frank added. "The first thing we do tomorrow is airmail that arrowhead to Dad's friend, Mr Hopewell, in Chicago. He'll be able to identify it. He's a specialist in primitive weapons."

Storing the packet of ashes and the lantern slides in their small safe, the boys returned to the house and tiptoed up to their bedroom.

"I'd like to get up early to work on this mystery," Frank said drowsily.

"Me too." Joe set the alarm for six and switched off the light. A few moments later both boys were sleeping soundly.

"Gosh," Joe exclaimed, when he heard the rasping buzz of the alarm, "I feel as though I'd just gone to bed!"

"You did practically," Frank muttered as he sat upright and blinked.

Then both boys dropped back on their pillows and fell asleep again. It was eight o'clock when they again awoke and the brothers grinned sheepishly.

"Mm, I smell bacon and eggs!" Joe said, and got out of bed in a hurry.

"What are you boys up to now?" Aunt Gertrude asked them as she passed the crisp bacon and honey buns.

They gave an account of the curios, the missile, the chase, and the events at the museum.

Breakfast was almost over when the telephone rang.

"Wonder who's calling," Mrs Hardy said.

"Might be Fenton," Aunt Gertrude suggested.

"Or Mr Scath," Frank said.

"I'll get it," Joe offered, pushing back his chair. He disappeared into the hallway.

"Hello," Joe said cheerily.

"Hello, Joe," replied the excited voice of Tony Prito. "Valez has just phoned again!"

"What did he say?"

"Joe, he threatened you and Frank!"

∎ 5 ∎ Missing Valuables

"FRANK and I are being threatened by Valez!" Joe cried. "Why, Tony?"

"Valez says that you're interfering with my selling him the collection. I told him you had nothing to do with it. I wouldn't sell it, anyway. Boy, was he mad!

Threatened to make me give him whatever he wanted and said if you fellows didn't keep out of it he'd get you too!"

"How in the world does Valez know Frank and me?" Joe asked.

"I don't know," Tony replied, "but he called you 'those Hardy boys.'"

When Frank heard the threat a few minutes later, he began to speculate on what action they should take next to learn more about Valez.

"Now listen to me," Aunt Gertrude interrupted. "You'd better pay attention to that warning. There's just no sense in waiting until danger's right on top of you. If I were your parents—"

The front-door bell sounded and the lecture ended. As Frank started for the front of the house Joe followed, grinning.

Frank opened the front door. A tall, broad-shouldered stranger with red hair, who appeared to be a merchant seaman, was standing on the porch. Several tattoo marks covered his thick, bared forearms. As he took a step forward, the boys, suspecting that he might be an agent of Valez, braced themselves in the doorway and eyed the visitor.

"Good morning," Frank said politely. "What can we do for you?"

"You're the Hardy boys?"

"Yes."

A broad smile creased the young man's face. Awkwardly he fingered his crew cut. Then he extended a sun-tanned hand to the brothers.

"My name is Wortman," he began in a voice that seemed no less friendly than his handshake. "I've been lookin' for you for some time."

Joe asked the man to come into the house. "Don't mind if I do," Wortman replied. "It's quite a walk from the Bayport station."

This answer puzzled the boys. They had guessed from his clothing that he had come from some ship docked at Bayport.

"Did you arrive here this morning?" Joe asked, as they entered the living-room and he swung a chair round for the caller.

"Yes, I came from New York on the sleeper," the man replied.

"You came all that way just to see us, Mr Wortman?" Joe asked incredulously.

"Well, indirectly," Wortman began. "But first, let's quit this 'Mister' stuff. My name's Willie and that's what you're to call me."

"Okay, Willie." Joe smiled. "I still want to know why you'd travel all the way here from New York just to see us."

Wortman explained that he was an able-bodied seaman on a freighter plying to Central and South America. At the mention of these last words Joe and Frank exchanged glances.

Wortman, noticing their sudden interest, asked, "Anything unusual about a fellow shippin' to South America?"

"Oh, no," Joe replied hastily. "Nothing at all."

"Well," Wortman continued, "my ship docked in New York last week. After I was paid off, I went to visit an old shopkeeper friend of mine—a man named Roberto Prito."

"Prito!" Frank repeated. The name had startled him, but he restrained himself from showing this.

"Yes," Wortman went on. "But my friend had died

and his shop was locked tight. I sure felt bad—he was a good pal." After a pause the seaman continued. "I was disappointed, too, because I'd hoped to pick up two medallions there—one the size of a half dollar, the other somewhat larger.

"I heard from a neighbour of Roberto's that a large shipment of objects from the shop had been sent to Tony Prito here in Bayport. Figuring the medallions might been have in the shipment, I came on out. I went to Tony's house as soon as I got off the train. He says he's pretty sure they're not in the collection. Tony had to take the truck out on a rush job for his dad, so he advised me to come here and talk to you about them."

"Did these two medallions belong to you?" Frank asked.

"Yes," Wortman replied. "I got them from a buddy of mine who has since been killed. A short time ago, when I was broke, I pawned them with Roberto."

"And you were trying to buy them back?" Frank asked.

"Y-yes." His halting reply puzzled the brothers. Wortman went on, "I guess I may be a bit foolish about goin' to such trouble to locate them. They're really of no value to anyone else. I'd just like to get hold of them for the sake of sentiment—something to remember my friend by."

"Can you tell us more about their appearance?" Frank asked.

Wortman explained that the medallions were made of some kind of cheap metal, and had a design of curving lines. In addition, the larger one had a fake opal set in it, while the other had the word *Texichapi* inscribed on it.

"What does that mean?" Joe asked.

"I don't know," the seaman answered.

"You must understand," Frank said, "that even if we do find them, we wouldn't have the authority to hand over the medallions to you immediately. We'd have to return them to Tony, then you'd have to make arrangements with him."

"That's fair enough," the visitor replied.

Wortman rose from his chair, and after thanking the boys, started for the door. Suddenly he stopped.

"There's one other thing," he said. "I was told by a man in a seaport down on the Gulf that there's a curse connected with these medallions."

"A curse!" Joe exclaimed.

"The man told me that trouble will come to anyone who sells these objects," Wortman explained. "That's the real reason why I want to get them back."

The boys drove Wortman to the station and watched him board the train for New York, then they returned home to finish their breakfast. They reviewed for their mother and aunt in careful detail the whole story Wortman had told them.

"How much of it was trumped up?" Joe asked his brother.

"Surely the part about the curse," Frank replied. "I believe Willie's imagination got the better of him at that stage. But for the rest, it sounds real enough."

"Do you think that there is any connection between these medallions and the episode at the museum—the intruder and the embers in the coffin?" Joe queried.

"I sure do," said Frank. "Maybe the intruder believes the story of the curse and was trying to break it."

As Joe poured a glass of milk, he suddenly recalled that Aunt Gertrude's lecture on their sleuthing had been interrupted by Wortman's visit. "As you were saying," he joked, "we should give up chasing danger."

"Why," Miss Hardy snapped, ignoring the remark, "you boys can't even eat your breakfast in peace. You go running off with total strangers in the middle of a meal."

"We do that just to work up an appetite," Joe said, reaching for another bun. "There's nothing like a little road work between courses."

At that moment, Frank, who had been lost in thought, interrupted his aunt and brother to suggest that there was another lead to follow.

"We might inquire from Mr Cosgrove at the New York bank that's acting as executor of Roberto Prito's will, if he's come across these medallions."

"Good idea, Frank, but Tony ought to be the one to do it," Joe said.

A few minutes after they had been in touch with Tony, their friend called back. He said the bank had reported that there was no record of the two medallions.

Where could they be? What had Roberto Prito done with these items? Had he sold them?

The boys' discussion was halted when their mother called that Mr Hardy was on the telephone. "Hurry! He's phoning from New York."

"Wait till he hears about our latest mystery!" Joe exclaimed.

Mr Hardy told his sons news of general interest about his work, then said, "I had a case that sounded baffling, but I had to turn it down because I'm too busy. Upon the recommendation of a detective agency here, an Alberto Torres called on me at my hotel.

"He claimed to be the head of a Guatemalan

THE CLUE IN THE EMBERS

patriotic society," Mr Hardy explained. "He says that his group is trying to uncover a treasure, the location of which they suspect is known by some unscrupulous persons who are trying to steal it. Naturally, the treasure belongs to the government."

"Maybe Frank and I could work on the case until you'd be ready to take over," Joe said enthusiastically. "Did Torres give you any clues?"

"He said that their only clue is a couple of medallions which have disappeared," Mr Hardy answered.

"Medallions!" Joe exclaimed, and quickly related what had happened in the famous detective's absence. Mr Hardy listened intently and told Joe that he would try at once to contact Torres.

"Hang up," he said, "and I'll call you back as soon as I've talked with him."

Minutes passed. Finally the phone rang.

"Bad luck," the boys' father reported. "Torres checked out of his hotel and left no forwarding address."

"Can't we do something about finding him?" Frank asked. "Maybe he's going to contact Willie Wortman in New York City."

His father agreed that this was a possibility but said that he had to leave for Washington on another case. He suggested that the boys fly to New York and check again with the bank's records regarding the curios. There might be a tie-in between the two men interested in the medallions. Perhaps they could pick up a clue on Torres and Wortman.

"What does Torres look like?" Frank asked.

"Short, slender, dark. He has a prominent chin and a black moustache."

"That description fits the blowgun man!" Frank exclaimed.

Mr Hardy said that it couldn't be the same man because Torres had been talking to him in New York at the time the missile had been fired at Joe.

An hour later Frank, Joe, and Tony were winging towards New York on a double mission.

"Where should we start work?" Joe asked.

"First thing to do," Frank suggested, "is to call on Mr Cosgrove and get his permission to check through the list ourselves. There's a good chance that he may have overlooked something."

At the bank the boys were received cordially by Mr Cosgrove and another man who was assisting him in the execution of the Prito estate. The trio was given permission to investigate the shopkeeper's private records. In the cool vault of the bank building the boys began their examination with the help of Mr Cosgrove. Page after page was eagerly scanned in a search for the two items that might have escaped the bankers' eyes.

Finding nothing, the boys turned to a diary and quickly looked over the notations. "Here's something of interest!" Joe exclaimed. He pointed to an entry written in a fine hand. "I'll read it to you.

"It says, first of all, that Roberto Prito did buy the medallions from Willie Wortman."

"That confirms part of Willie's story," Frank said.

"And according to this diary," Joe continued, "they were actually in the possession of Tony's uncle when he died. But now listen. In a separate notation it says, 'These medallions seem old and valuable. The strange design may indicate they are a clue to something. I will study them later.'"

"Mr Cosgrove," Frank said abruptly, "may we look over Mr Prito's store?"

"Of course. I'll get the key for you from the safe-deposit box."

"Torres can wait," Joe said excitedly as the banker went off. "Let's try to find the medallions or the reason why they've disappeared!"

Twenty minutes later they were inserting the key into the padlock of the late Roberto Prito's shop in a Greenwich Village street. Pending settlement of the estate, it had not been re-rented.

"I'll lead the way," Tony said. "I know where the office is."

Bolting the door on the inside, the trio started for the rear of the empty shop, now dimly lighted by the late afternoon sun. Joe followed close behind Tony towards a small office.

Frank, a few strides behind, noticed an unusual looking showcase standing at an odd angle. His detecting instincts aroused, he moved the case and dropped to his knees. At first glance the floor boards under it looked the same as the others. But after a few moments of intent study Frank thought he could see the outline of what might be a trap door.

"Maybe there's a secret cellar under here!" he thought excitedly.

He tried to pull up the boards with his fingers. Failing, Frank pressed each board separately.

A moment later the whole section suddenly caved in. Frank lost his balance and crashed downwards into inky blackness!

·6· *Mr Bones*

Pitching headlong into the dark cellar below the shop of Tony's deceased uncle, Frank struck his head sharply against a packing case. He fell on to the concrete floor, unconscious!

In the store above, Tony had led Joe into the small office at the rear of the long room. A high partition darkened this section of the shop. Tony switched on a light.

"Where's Frank?" he asked.

"He was right behind me—" Joe began, looking out of the office door. "What could have happened?"

"Frank!" Tony called. "Frank, where are you?" His voice echoed emptily.

Retracing their steps, the two boys peered into the street. Frank was not in sight.

"It's just as if he were swallowed up in the—" Joe suddenly had an idea and began to look for an opening in the floor. He spotted the black rectangle behind the showcase.

"Look!" he cried. "A trap door! Frank must have fallen through." He called his brother's name but there was no response.

From his coat pocket Joe took the small flashlight he always carried and beamed it below.

"There he is!" Joe gasped. "I've got to get down and help him! Must be a ladder here somewhere."

He beamed his light under the flooring and found a

38

short ladder hinged flat under the floor. Unhooking it, he let the ladder down. Both boys scampered below.

Using precaution in case of broken bones, Joe checked Frank's condition. "Wind's knocked out of him," he told Tony a moment later, "and he has a nasty bruise on his head, but I guess that's all."

As Joe spoke, Frank moved for the first time. He shook his head and made an attempt to sit up.

"Take it easy, fellow," Joe warned him.

With the boys' assistance Frank climbed to his feet. "What hit me?" he asked dazedly.

Tony raised the beam of his flashlight to the trap door and explained what had happened. Revived, but still somewhat groggy, Frank started for the ladder. "Guess I touched a secret spring," he said.

"Just a second," Tony said. "Let's take a look in these packing cases. We may find something interesting."

Near him on the floor lay a claw hammer. Tony prised open a single board on each of the cases. "Here's something I didn't see on the lists." He held up a small antique statuette of a Chinese horseman.

"Mr Cosgrove evidently doesn't know about these boxes," Joe remarked.

Tony was excited. "This may be the answer to the missing medallions," he said. "Let's look through them."

But Joe, seeing that Frank was not steady on his feet, suggested that they postpone searching the crates and look for a hotel where his brother could rest and recover from the accident.

"We'll return tomorrow and investigate this cellar with Mr Cosgrove," Tony said.

Before they left, Joe examined the trap door, and

discovering how the hidden spring worked, closed it. Then the boys locked up and departed.

After getting settled in their hotel room, Tony phoned Mr Cosgrove and it was arranged that he and his associate would accompany the boys to the shop the next morning. The bank knew nothing about the cellar room, he said, and the curios stored there had not been listed.

Meanwhile, Frank had undressed. Joe said to him, "I think Tony and I will do a little looking around town for Torres while you relax."

Joe asked at the information desk in the foyer for a list of hotels in New York where Central Americans might go to be with other Spanish-speaking people, then he and Tony set out. It was several hours later when they returned.

Frank said he was feeling fine and asked what they had learned.

"Nothing," Joe reported. "Torres has probably left town."

After a hearty breakfast the next morning, the boys returned to the Prito shop. Mr Cosgrove and his assistant, named Jones, arrived a short time later and the examination of the secret cellar began. They opened crate after crate.

"It appears that Mr Prito stored his queerest objects here," Mr Cosgrove remarked, after several cases had been unpacked and revealed an array of skulls, animal teeth, an Egyptian toy ferry and all kinds of odd theatrical costumes.

"That's why I think there's a good chance of our finding the medallions here," said Tony. "The notation my uncle made proves that he didn't consider the medallions just routine curios."

Working methodically, the group had almost completed the inventory by noon. But there was no sign of the mysterious medallions.

"I'm afraid that you're going to be disappointed about them," said Mr Cosgrove as he wrote down the final item on his long list. "For you, Tony, this has been a very profitable morning, but unless your uncle had another hiding place that we haven't discovered, it would seem as if the medallions are gone."

Mr Cosgrove picked up his lists and started for the ladder. The others followed one by one to the main floor. Frank, the last to leave, reluctantly set his foot on the bottom rung. Could there be another hiding place? he mused. Stopping, he played his flashlight slowly back and forth along the solid walls of the cramped storage space.

Suddenly he saw, about eight feet from the floor, a faint series of slits that formed a rectangle in the wall. Quickly he stepped down, clambered over some cases, and ran his hand along the wooden slits. Tapping with his knuckles, he heard the hollow sound of space behind the rectangle.

"Looks like the transom of a door," Frank thought. "The door has been sealed off."

With his thumbnail he tried to prise open the thin section. "I'll need a chisel," he decided.

His heart pounding, Frank scrambled up the ladder and cried out his discovery to the others.

"It looks as if it might be a secret passage!" he exclaimed as he looked for a chisel. Finding one in a rusted tool chest in a drawer of the office desk, Frank led the others back into the cellar.

"This beats me!" Mr Cosgrove exclaimed as Frank's flashlight outlined the rectangle in the wall. "How could we have missed this?" The executor chuckled. "I can see how you Hardys have earned such a fine reputation as detectives."

Frank climbed on to a packing case and started testing the section with the sharp edge of the chisel while Joe held the flashlight. The first attempts failed. Then, as he moved the tool to a spot along the right vertical line, he felt the whole section tremble.

"It's coming!" he cried out. Again he forced the cutting tool into the slit, got a stronger bite, and wrenched the partition open. Dropping the chisel, he gripped the wood with his strong fingers and tugged the whole partition free from its position.

"Jumpin' Jehoshaphat!" Frank cried. He almost fell off the packing case as he reared back from the sight that met his eyes.

"What is it?" Joe asked.

Frank thrust one arm into the opening. Slowly he dragged out a human skeleton! Its white ghostliness at first shocked the group into silence.

Then, as Joe realized it was a medical specimen, his humour came to the rescue. "A room-mate for you, Tony." He grinned.

Frank lowered the skeleton to Tony, who gingerly placed it on a packing case. "I just remembered something," he said. "My uncle was very superstitious about skeletons. I guess he didn't plan on our finding this fellow. Anybody who wants this bag of bones can have him!"

"How about giving him to a medical school?" Mr Cosgrove suggested.

After making several calls from the office, he said that a small private institution would be glad to accept the specimen. He gave the boys directions to the medical school, adding, "Tony, will you leave the key to the shop at the bank when you're through with it? And I hope you find those medallions." The executors bade the boys good-bye.

"Who wants to carry Mr Bones to his next place of residence?" Tony asked. "I'll give up the pleasure. He's not my type!"

Joe looked at his brother. "He can sit on our lap while we ride there. After all, you found him."

Grinning, Frank said, "Guess I'm really stuck." He clutched the skeleton and started climbing the ladder. The others followed him up and Joe stepped out on to the sidewalk to hail a taxi.

Placing Mr Bones on the outside of the seat next to Frank, the group headed for the medical school. They had gone only a block when a police siren sounded behind them!

·7· *A Street Chase*

"THE motorcycle cop is after *us!*" Frank exclaimed. "He must have seen the skeleton!"

The sound of the siren grew louder and the taxi was ordered to pull over to the kerb. The policeman, a big, red-faced man, climbed off his motorcycle and walked slowly back to the taxi. He stared at Mr Bones.

"Where'd that come from?" he roared.

"We—we found him in a cellar," Tony explained, feeling a little foolish.

"Breakin' an' enterin'," the cop accused. "Driver, where did you pick up these fellows?"

The driver said that they had hailed him at Prito's Curio Shop.

"So!" the policeman exclaimed, looking stern. "That shop's locked up. I knew old Prito well. You fellows have got some explainin' to do."

Tony suddenly recalled that in his pocket was a letter from Mr Cosgrove. "Just a minute, officer. I can explain everything to you." He pulled out the letter and handed it over. The burly policeman read the paper, eyed Tony, then handed it back.

"So you're a Prito!" he exclaimed. "Now that I look at you, I can see you're like Roberto. Same snappy black eyes."

The boys breathed more easily. The cop began to laugh. "Just to show that my heart's in the right place, I'll give Billy Bones here an escort as far as the end of my beat." He gunned his motorcycle out ahead of the taxi and headed for the East River Drive. There, the policeman slowed down.

"Good-bye!" he called as he made a U-turn and left them.

The taxi droned on its way. Twenty blocks north the driver pulled into a side street and drew up to a white cement building.

As the taxi disappeared into the city traffic, the boys walked through the hospital doorway. A young intern who passed them grinned. "Who's your air-conditioned pal?" he cracked.

The boys chuckled and walked to a desk where a nurse was on duty. The pleasant woman, about fifty years old, smiled as the group approached her, four abreast.

The nurse directed the boys to the school, across a wide centre court. There, a genial white-haired physician welcomed Mr Bones and thanked the boys.

As the trio walked down the hospital steps, Tony said, "Are we going back to Bayport now? We have a plane reservation, you know."

"That's right," said Frank. "Well, I guess there's not much chance of finding Torres, so we may as well leave."

"We must return the shop key to Mr Cosgrove," Tony reminded them.

At the bank the boys were told that the newly found curios were being appraised at the shop and Tony could take any of them he wished. After lunch the boys brought their bags from the hotel and stuffed several of the smaller objects into them.

"We'd better hurry," Tony observed. "Our plane leaves in less than an hour."

He called a taxi and the boys headed for the airport. As it stopped at a busy intersection near the East River, Frank suddenly gripped his brother's arm. "Look!" he cried. "Over there on the sidewalk. Willie Wortman!"

The recent visitor to the Hardy home appeared to be walking with another man. Wortman's broad shoulders partially blocked his companion from view. But as the taxi passed them, Joe caught a glimpse of the other man's face. He was dark-haired and black-moustached.

"Say, he could be the blowgun man or Torres!" Frank exclaimed. "Come on. We're getting off right here!"

"We'll miss our plane," Tony protested.

"We'll catch the next one," Joe replied.

The light turned green and the taxi started up.

"Hold it, driver!" Frank called, and the man pulled to the kerb. "We're getting out."

Frank paid him and the boys got out. "Tony, you stay here with the suitcases," Frank instructed. "Joe and I will talk to Willie."

"Okay," Tony agreed. He pushed the three bags into a pile and watched his pals dash through the crowd after the two men who had crossed the street.

The moustached stranger had now dropped slightly behind Wortman. As the boys hurried after them, the pair turned up a side street.

The brothers dodged through the crowd. The red-haired sailor seemed to be walking with unconcern, but the other man glanced from side to side uneasily. He acted almost as if he feared someone were trailing him.

Willie Wortman suddenly looked back. Catching sight of the boys, he called out, "Frank and Joe Hardy!" The moustached man also glanced back, then he broke into a run.

Frank stayed to speak to the sailor while Joe continued the chase after the stranger. But the man, having a head start, ran through an alley leading to another street. Joe lost the trail completely. Disappointed, he walked back to where his brother was talking to Wortman.

"What are you fellows doin' here in the city?" the seaman was saying. He did not seem at all curious as to where Joe had been.

"Just came up for a short visit," Frank replied noncommittally. "We were on our way to the airport when we saw you. Have you any news about the medallions? We haven't found anything."

Wortman shook his head. "No luck so far."

The brothers said nothing about the other man.

Neither of them was absolutely certain that he had been with Wortman, nor that he was the blowgun suspect.

Before the Hardys had a chance to learn if Willie had been alone, the sailor said, "I'll be glad when I ship out on another voyage. It's sure lonely in New York when you don't know anyone." Turning to Frank, he said, "Don't forget about the medallions. That curse business is getting under my skin. You know what? I think it might have been the cause of old Mr Prito's death!"

"That's ridiculous," Frank told him. "And stop worrying about the curse."

"I'll try," Wortman promised.

The boys assured him that they would keep on searching for the medallions, then Joe said, "Sorry to have kept you from your friend."

"Friend?" Willie asked, a puzzled look on his face.

The Hardys exchanged glances. If the suspected man had been with him, didn't Willie want to admit it? Or, perhaps, had the moustached man been following the seaman unknown to him? At this moment it seemed as if the latter possibility were true, so they did not pursue the subject. The boys said good-bye and returned to Tony.

"Didn't learn a thing," Frank said. He hailed another cab and once they were inside, told Tony about their brief conversation with Wortman.

When they arrived at the airport, the boys were informed that they had just missed the flight to Bayport. There would be a two-hour wait for the next plane.

"Hold on!" Frank exclaimed, as they stood trying to decide what to do. "Looks like George Simons over there near that new four-seater job."

"It's George and nobody else!" Joe agreed. "I wonder if he's heading for Bayport."

George Simons was a close friend of Mr Hardy. He owned a helicopter and several small planes. Frank got permission from a gatekeeper to run out and talk to Simons.

"Frank Hardy!" the flier exclaimed. "Are you snoopin' for clues in the big city?"

"Yes." Frank smiled. "And we've just missed the flight back home."

"You didn't miss this one." George grinned. "I'm about to take off. Are you alone?"

Frank explained that Joe and Tony Prito were with him.

"Perfect!" George said heartily. "Three and one is four. Get your gang together and let's go."

It was late afternoon when the plane circled the Bayport field and landed. The boys drove back to town in the Hardy's convertible with Frank at the wheel.

As Tony got out, Joe removed the curios from the Hardys' bags and helped his friend carry his luggage and the other articles to the front door.

At seven-thirty the morning of the second day after their return from New York, the boys were shaken out of a sound sleep by a frantic hammering at the front door.

"Who's there?" Joe called through the screened bedroom window.

A figure ran on to the lawn. It was Chet Morton. "Hurry out!" he cried.

Frank and Joe raced down the stairs and flung open the door.

"Look!" Chet said breathlessly, pointing.

On the floor of the porch a foot from the railing stood a six-inch-high, cone-shaped pile of ashes!

·8· *A Suspicious Barber*

THE mysterious enemy's latest warning struck fear into Chet's heart. "This must be the work of that fire guy in the museum!" the chubby boy exclaimed. "And now he's—he's threatening you both personally."

"We've already been threatened personally," Frank replied. He told of the warning Tony had been given by Valez over the phone. "And this makes me think Valez was the person in the museum."

"Maybe he's putting a curse on you," Chet quavered. "The—the medallion curse!"

"Could be," Frank agreed, smiling. "But he may find it'll backfire."

As Joe and Chet watched, Frank got a small box and swept the ashes into it. "I'll get dressed and then take these to our lab and analyze them. You fellows may as well start breakfast. I smell blueberry muffins baking."

Chet was eating his sixth muffin by the time Frank returned. Dashing into the room he announced that the photomicrographs showed the burned material to be bones!

"Human bones!" Chet almost choked on the muffin. "Ugh, maybe this is a warning that we'll all be roasted alive by some lunatic!"

"Take it easy, Chet." Frank grinned. "The bones were from a chicken."

As Chet took another muffin, Joe slyly remarked that it was strange how the magic of food worked on

49

their friend. "You don't seem to be afraid of anything now."

"That's not quite true," Chet replied, grinning. "I'm afraid we'll run out of muffins!"

After the meal Chet went on his way to buy the tractor part. Joe phoned Tony to tell him about the latest warning and to find out if he had had any further word from Valez.

"Not a peep," Tony answered. "Do you think he's the one who left the ashes on your porch?"

"If he was," Frank replied, "it means he's still in Bayport. Want to come on a search for Valez?"

"You bet. Why don't you pick me up?"

The three boys spent the entire day sleuthing. After consulting the police records and learning nothing, they went to hotels, motels, boarding-houses and real-estate agencies. No one could give them a lead.

"There's one place in Bayport we haven't investigated," Frank remarked. "The new development on the edge of town. People are moving there every day and hardly know one another yet. If there's any place where a stranger could live unnoticed, that would be it!"

"Of course!" Joe agreed instantly. "Let's go!"

The boys cruised in their convertible through the recently paved streets of the development, looking for any Spanish-type person.

"I don't recognize anyone," Joe remarked, as they drove past adults and children working or playing on their front lawns. "And I haven't seen a glimpse of the Latin type of person we're looking for."

As the car pulled out of the development around five-thirty and turned on to the highway, Tony suddenly cried out:

"Stop! There's the name Valez!"

On the front window of a barber shop, occupying the corner of a new block of stores, the name S. VALEZ was stamped in large gold letters! Parking the car, the boys headed for the shop. The screen door was locked.

In the rear of the establishment they saw a dark-haired man sitting hunched over a small desk. He appeared to be writing. Frank knocked on the door. The man swung round abruptly.

"Too late!" he called in a nervous voice. "Come back tomorrow. Shop is closed."

"Are you Mr Valez?" Frank asked.

"Yes," the barber replied. "What do you want?"

"Not a haircut," Frank replied and said they had come to get some information from him.

This statement seemed to upset the man. "What kind?" he sputtered. "I am a good man. I come from Spain. Everything legal. You boys hoodlums? Since I came here I've heard a lot about holdups. Please, I have no money."

Hastily Frank assured Mr Valez that they were not going to rob him. To himself Frank said, "He's from Spain. This can't be our man."

The barber relaxed and smiled. He walked forward and began to talk freely, though he did not unlock the door. Mr Valez asked what he could do to help the boys. His straightforward answers quickly convinced them that he was above suspicion.

The barber explained that he had been in this country only a short time and had not met anyone else of the same name. Then he excused himself, saying he was writing a letter to his mother in Spain and wanted to catch the outgoing evening airmail. The boys thanked him and left.

"Only one Valez in town and he's not our man," moaned Tony, as they let him off at his house.

The Hardys drove to Elm Street, turned into their driveway, and put the car away. When they entered the kitchen, Joe found a pinned-up note near the refrigerator telling them that Mrs Hardy and her sister-in-law had gone out for dinner and the evening. The boys' dinner was on the stove, ready for warming. Also, their father had phoned to say he was still in Washington but might be home later that evening.

"Let's turn on the TV news before we eat," Frank said, and the brothers headed for the living-room. As Joe led the way through the dining-room, he stopped in his tracks. Then he pointed to the floor, crying, "Look at those sideboard drawers!"

The four large drawers had been pulled out and their contents dumped out. Silverware and linen lay scattered on the floor.

"A burglary!" Joe exclaimed.

The brothers dashed into the living-room and the hall. These, too, were a shambles!

•9• *An Amazing Discovery*

FRANK and Joe ran through the house. From top to bottom every drawer in the place had been pulled out and rifled with one exception. The locked files in Mr Hardy's study had not been broken into, probably because they had a secret combination.

"Joe," said Frank presently, "do you realize that nothing seems to be missing? Not silver, jewellery, or anything valuable. What *was* the housebreaker after?"

"Something he didn't find, that's sure."

Frank had just about concluded that the mysterious person was connected with one of their father's cases rather than their own when an idea suddenly occurred to him. He hurried back to the brothers' bedroom.

"I know what that fellow was after and he got it!" Frank called as he opened his cupboard door.

Joe dashed in. The cigarette-type box from Tony's collection of curios was missing from the closet shelf. "But why would anyone break in here just to carry off that worthless box!" he exclaimed.

"Perhaps it wasn't so worthless after all," Frank reflected. He was about to add something else when his speculating was interrupted by the arrival of Mrs Hardy and Aunt Gertrude in a friend's car. As the boys ran downstairs to tell what had happened, Joe remarked, "Guess they decided to come home right after dinner."

The two women were alarmed when Frank told them what had happened, but a quick investigation by the women showed that no articles were missing.

"Except for our curio box," said Joe.

Aunt Gertrude blushed with embarrassment. "Oh, that box!" she said. "Maybe it wasn't stolen after all!" Her announcement surprised the boys as much as their earlier discovery of the ransacking.

"What do you mean?" Frank asked her, mystified.

"If the burglar didn't take it," she replied sheepishly, "the box is inside my sewing machine. I borrowed it this afternoon to use for a button box. I didn't think you'd mind."

"Of course not, Aunty," Frank replied. "But it's possible that we've been underrating that object. Will you see if it's still there?"

The box was found, exactly where the chagrined woman had placed it—not in a drawer but down inside the covered sewing-machine. Frank and Joe teased their aunt, telling her how glad they were that it had been she, and not the housebreaker, who had taken the curio.

"I think we'd better look this over," said Frank. "It might be the object of the man's search."

"What makes you think so?" Mrs Hardy asked.

Frank laughed. "Aunt Gertrude's button box may be more valuable than we thought. Don't forget, it's the only souvenir we own from Tony's collection. The intruder at the museum might have seen Mr Scath hand me the box, and knowing its worth, came searching for it."

"That sounds reasonable," his mother agreed.

Frank eyed the curio for a moment, then asked, "Do you folks realize what this is made of? It looks like Central American mahogany! The same as the charred bits we analyzed."

"What!" Aunt Gertrude exclaimed.

Frank was examining the box carefully and now using pressure on each side of it to see if the curio had a secret compartment. "It has a fake bottom!" he exclaimed triumphantly a moment later, sliding it off.

Then, with his thumbnail, Frank prised out a thin piece of wood built in above the bottom of the box. In it was wedged a large, engraved golden coin! Eagerly he took out the piece and held it up.

"One of the medallions!" Joe exclaimed. "And it

looks like real gold. Boy, am I glad that burglar didn't find it!"

"And see!" Frank cried. "It has the large opal set in it that Wortman told us about!" The stone was set on one of the lines that crossed the medallion. It was a beautiful opal, not a cheap one as Wortman had stated.

"Tony's uncle thought it had a special meaning," Frank said. "I have an idea that these engraved lines may form a map of some kind."

"What was it Wortman said was on the other medallion?" Joe asked.

"It was a word," his brother replied. "Sounded like Texichapi."

As Mrs Hardy and Aunt Gertrude examined the gold coin, Joe said, "Maybe these engraved lines show the exact spot where some treasure is buried in Texichapi! Remember what Torres told Dad."

"Let's look up Texichapi," Frank suggested, and went for the atlas. The boys studied the entire area from Mexico to the tip of South America. Their search yielded nothing. Nor was there any place in the world with that name.

"Apparently," Frank concluded, "Texichapi means something else. What about it being a secret password?"

"Maybe," spoke up Mrs Hardy, a dreamy expression in her eyes. "But it could be the name of a person. Some ancient king buried with a ransom in jewels."

Aunt Gertrude snorted. "Huh! Sounds more to me like one of those peppery fire-spitting South American recipes!" she exclaimed.

Everyone laughed and Frank said, "Probably the answer to the riddle depends on having both medallions. In the meanwhile, I think we ought to memorize the exact position of these lines and where the opal is placed."

"Good idea," Joe said.

"While you're doing that," said Mrs Hardy, "I'll warm up your supper."

The boys concentrated on the lines for several minutes, then tried drawing them from memory on paper. It was necessary for both Frank and Joe to do this again and again until they had memorized the lines perfectly.

While the brothers ate a late supper, Mrs Hardy remarked that she thought they ought to notify the police of the attempted burglary.

"I know that as detectives you would like to solve this yourself, but as proper-acting citizens of Bayport we're bound to report it," she insisted. "What kind of law and order would we have if people didn't notify the police when their homes were broken into?"

"You're right," her sons agreed. As Frank arose from the table and was about to call headquarters, the telephone rang.

"I'll take it," Aunt Gertrude called from the hall. A moment later she said, "It's Fenton! He's on his way home. Says he wants someone to meet him at the airport at nine o'clock."

"I'll go," the brothers chorused, then Frank said, "You pick him up, Joe. Drop me at the police station and I'll talk to Captain Collig personally."

"How about this medallion?" Joe asked. "Don't you think we ought to give it to Tony? After all, it belongs to him."

"You're right. Take it along and show Dad, then leave it at Tony's."

Putting the medallion into his pocket, Joe started for

the garage. Frank followed directly and the brothers set off on their double errand.

"Whatever you do," Frank warned as he hopped out at the police station, "watch yourself."

Joe headed the car towards the airport. Halfway there he remembered that the main road was cut off because of road repairs. That meant he would have to take the lonely one that led past the museum.

The night was warm and the air still. "Like the one when we brought Tony's stuff out to the museum," Joe thought as the convertible purred along. He came to the building and slowed up. "Most of Tony's inheritance is in there now. But the most valuable piece may be the medallion I have," he mused, fingering the outline of the object in his sports shirt pocket.

As he drove along, there were fewer trees and the countryside became flatter. "About one more mile and I'll be at the field. It'll be great to see Dad and tell him first-hand all the new developments," Joe said to himself.

The road took a long bend to the right and then straightened out. As the car approached the highway, its headlights picked up a frightening sight. Several yards ahead a man lay at the edge of the road. Joe wondered if he was the victim of a hit-and-run driver.

The brakes screeched as he slowed his car. Near the prostrate figure, another person staggered forward, shielding his face from the glare of the headlights and signalled Joe to stop.

"What happened?" the Hardy boy asked, as he jumped out to help.

"Don't know," the man who had signalled mumbled in reply. Now Joe could dimly see his face—enough to learn that he had a moustache.

Suddenly the roadside victim leaped to his feet. He too shielded his face so completely that Joe could see nothing of it but his eyes.

Too late Joe realized that this was a trap. He tried to jump back into the car, but the man nearest him let go a powerful blow that sent Joe reeling against the wing.

Recovering his balance, Joe lashed out at his assailant, but the next instant the other man struck a blow from behind. Quick as lightning, Joe whirled and connected with a smash that sent his adversary sprawling on the pavement.

If only a car would come by, there might be some hope for him. But none did.

"If I could get back behind the wheel, I'd have a chance to drive away!" Joe thought desperately.

He got one foot inside the car, but his assailants closed in again. They yanked him out and twisted his arms.

"Let go, you goons!" he cried out in pain.

He managed to tear away from their grip for a second, but one of the thugs shot a smashing blow to his chin. Joe blacked out!

When he came to seconds later his mouth was gagged and a handkerchief was tied over his eyes. He was bound hand and foot, and lay in a thicket.

Joe realized that not once during the struggle had either of the men spoken a word. Even now, when a hand started to frisk his pockets, not a sound came from his enemies.

To Joe's dismay, he felt the hand go into the pocket that held the medallion!

·10· *The Peculiar Ping*

LYING bound and gagged in the underbrush off the highway, Joe struggled to loosen the cords that cut into his wrists. Somewhere nearby in the darkness, his assailants were talking. They seemed to be very excited. Joe strained to hear what they were saying.

"They're speaking Spanish!" he thought, catching a phrase or two of their chatter that he could understand. He heard one of them say, "Now we can find the place." A moment later the other broke out fiercely, "I want that fortune!"

The talk was suddenly drowned out by the sound of a car engine roaring to life. The men were leaving! Joe had not seen a car when he stopped to help the "victim." But now he realized the sound of the motor was different from that of the Hardy's convertible. The men probably had concealed their car in the thicket along the road.

Joe wondered how they knew he would be passing this very spot. He concluded that they must have been eavesdropping below the windows at the Hardy house when plans for going to the airport were being made.

He heard his own car being driven off the road into the brush and then came the sound of running feet as the driver returned to the getaway car. Next minute the car sped off.

"I didn't get a single clue, except that one of the

men had a moustache," Joe moaned. Suddenly, however, he recalled something. The sound of the getaway car's engine. It had a very strange *ping*!

Meanwhile, at the airport, the plane from Washington had landed, and Mr Hardy, a tall, handsome man in his forties, strode down the passenger gangway to the field. Looking hurriedly about for some member of his family and failing to see one, he started for the waiting room. "Perhaps they missed the announcement," he thought. But there was no sign of any of the Hardy family in the waiting room. Mr Hardy decided to wait a few minutes before phoning home.

Ten minutes later the detective inquired at the main desk if any call had come in for him before his arrival. Upon being told that none had, he hurried to the telephone and called home.

"Oh, Fenton," Mrs Hardy sighed, "I'm so glad to hear your voice and know that you're back!" She went on to tell of the attempted burglary. Suddenly she stopped, "But you've already heard this from Joe."

"Joe's not here," Mr Hardy replied gravely. "That's the reason I'm calling."

"But he left in plenty of time to meet you," Mrs Hardy said, worried. "Oh, dear, something terrible has happened. I just know it has."

Mr Hardy tried to console his upset wife, by saying that Joe might have had trouble with the car. Then he asked, "Is Frank there?"

Frank had just returned from his talk with Chief Collig. He came to the phone. "Hello, Dad."

"Frank, do you know what route Joe was taking out here?"

Frank told of the detour, adding that Joe would have had to use the lonely road past the Howard Museum.

"Dad, we found one of those medallions and Joe had it with him. Maybe he's been waylaid!"

Mr Hardy snorted. "I don't like the sound of this. Frank, take my car and start a search. I'll grab a taxi here and investigate from this end."

"Okay, Dad, I'll start right away."

Mr Hardy collected his luggage and hurried from the building. Hailing a taxi, he briefly told the driver, who knew him, what had happened, then directed the man to the spot where he and Frank were to meet.

"I've heard lots about the work you and your boys do, but I never thought I'd have a chance to get in on the detectin'. I would hate to have anything bad happen to one of you."

They set off along the highway over which there was now a heavy mist. Inch by inch they searched the roadsides with the taxi's spotlight, but there was no sign of Joe or the boys' convertible. Only one car came along from the opposite direction and the driver was not Frank. Discouraged, Mr Hardy finally drew near the spot where the attack had occured.

"Frank should be meeting me at any moment," Mr Hardy said to the driver, "unless he's found something."

At this moment the headlights of a car appeared from the direction of Bayport.

"This may be Frank. Blink your lights at him."

The taximan flicked his headlights several times and the approaching car answered the signal.

"Is that you, Dad?" Frank called as he pulled alongside.

"Yes. Any luck?"

"None. But I haven't examined the last hundred feet of roadside."

"Then we'll do that together," Mr Hardy called out. "Turn and move on slowly. We'll come directly behind you. Keep your spotlight on the left side of the highway. I'll watch the right."

Crawling at a snail's pace, the cars headed out along the highway. Over fifty feet had been covered with spotlights when suddenly Mr Hardy saw the glint of a shiny surface in some high bushes.

"Stop!" he told the driver. As the taxi backed slowly, the spotlight picked up the glint again. Revealed in the glare was the windshield of the boys' convertible.

"Blow your horn!" Mr Hardy directed. The cab's powerful horn blasted several times. Hearing the signal, Frank roared in reverse back to the taxi.

"I've got the spot on your car!" Mr Hardy cried.

Frank backed the saloon behind the taxi, leaped out, and, with his father, crashed through the brush. Quickly examining the convertible and the ground round it, they stood perplexed. There was no trace of Joe. But several sets of footprints were evident in the moist earth.

"Joe must have been ambushed," Mr Hardy said angrily. "And they've either kidnapped him or thrown him somewhere into this brush. We'll scour the whole area."

With flashlights, the two went on foot along both sides of the road, penetrating the clumps of underbrush. A few seconds later Frank discovered the trussed-up figure of his brother. Joe was still trying to fight free from his bonds and the gag in his mouth, but his efforts were feeble.

"Joe!" Frank cried out joyfully.

Yelling to his father, Frank knelt, removed the gag, and with his pocketknife severed the cords from

Joe's wrists and ankles. Exhausted from his ordeal and his mouth dry as paper, Joe could scarcely speak. But he whispered how glad he was to see his father and brother.

When they reached the taxi, the driver grinned. "I'm sure relieved that you're all right, boy. Whatever happened?" Realizing Joe could not talk easily, he reached under the seat and brought out a thermos bottle of water.

The water revived Joe considerably and he gave a sketchy account of the holdup but did not mention the stolen coin. Mr Hardy paid the taximan, included a generous extra amount for his time and trouble, and the man drove off.

"Now, Joe," Mr Hardy said. "I'm sure that there's more to your story. Are you up to telling us?"

Joe nodded, saying he felt much stronger. He told in detail about the ambush. "And now they have the medallion!" he moaned. "We've got to get it back for Tony! One of the men had a moustache. He might have been the blowgun man. There's just one other clue," and he explained about the *ping* in the enemies' engine.

"We'll notify the police at once," Mr Hardy declared. "We'll need as many men as possible to listen for that sound. If we act fast, there's an outside chance we can pick up those thugs."

Frank and Joe hurried to the convertible and their father to his saloon. Driving directly to police headquarters, Mr Hardy reported the incident. Chief Collig flashed this information over the teletype throughout the state. Then he assigned a patrolman to accompany the Hardys as they continued their search. The group, in Mr Hardy's saloon, stationed itself at various main streets and incoming roads to listen for the engine with the strange sound. For an hour they patrolled the town without success.

Then, at an intersection near the waterfront, Joe heard the peculiar *ping*! "That's the car!" he cried out. "After him, Dad!"

Mr Hardy turned round and sped after the car, which was now heading west.

"He's goin' at a pretty good clip!" the officer observed from the back seat. "You'd better open up and stop him!"

As the Hardy car closed the distance between the two cars, the driver of the other vehicle sensed that he was being pursued and instantly gunned his motor. But Mr Hardy manœuvred skilfully and soon caught up to the speeding car.

"Pull over!" the patrolman shouted as they passed the other vehicle.

The driver, realizing that he had no chance of getting away, slowed down and stopped at the side of the road. He was from out of town and confessed that he had stolen the car. Joe whispered that he was younger than either of the men who had held him up and did not speak with a Spanish accent. As the police officer left the Hardys to escort his prisoner to headquarters, Mr Hardy observed that they had helped the law, but so far as their case was concerned, they would have to continue their search.

"But that *ping*," Joe reiterated. "I'm certain it was the identical sound."

Frank felt that his brother's hunch should not be ignored. "I think we ought to follow the car down to the station and find out who owns it," Frank declared.

Mr Hardy agreed and drove back to headquarters.

The young prisoner was being booked when the Hardys arrived. Chief Collig waved to the Hardys as they entered.

"Thanks for helping us out," he said with his usual warm grin. "This seems to be a mighty popular auto. According to our list of stolen cars, this one was taken twice tonight!"

· 11 ·   A Shattered Window

"THERE goes our clue!" Joe exclaimed woefully when the Hardys learned that the car thief had "borrowed" the automobile from the two men who had originally stolen it.

The detective and his sons were assured by Chief Collig that he and the force would maintain a sharp lookout for Joe's Spanish-speaking assailants. Then the Hardys went home, where they continued discussing the mystery.

"Since the medallion was stolen and the only two people we know who are interested in it are Wortman and Torres," Mr Hardy said, "I think we'd better get on the trail of Torres."

"How about his patriotic society?" Frank asked. "Don't you think that's a phoney?"

"Probably," his father agreed. "We may solve this mystery if I play along with Torres, letting him believe that I think he's on the level."

"But," Joe put in, "if they've already discovered that you're our father, they won't retain your services."

"You forget," Mr Hardy replied, "that we're still

not certain who our arch-enemy really is. Is he Valez?
Torres? Wortman? Or someone else?"

"They may be working together," Joe ventured.

"I wonder," Frank commented, "if Torres is the
man who met Willie Wortman in the seaport and
learned about his having the medallions?"

"That could be," Mr Hardy agreed. "And Torres
might have made up the whole fantastic story about
the curse just to frighten Wortman into giving him the
medallions."

"Have you any idea where Torres might be?" Joe
asked, and told him of the unsuccessful sleuthing the
boys had done in New York.

"You've been reading my mind." Mr Hardy laughed.
"Before I turn in I'm going to phone a detective friend
of mine in New York and ask him to try tracking down
Torres. But since you ask, Joe, I'll tell you something."

"What is it?"

"I have a very strong suspicion," his father replied
slowly, "that our friend Torres may be right here in
Bayport!"

"Wow! What makes you think so?"

"Because I'm convinced Torres and Valez are
working together. If Torres is the boss, he probably
came here to see how his agent is doing."

Next morning, at breakfast, a special delivery letter
arrived from Chicago for Frank. "It's from your friend
Mr Hopewell, who analyzed the missile for us, Dad,"
he told Mr Hardy. Frank scanned the typewritten
sheet of information the expert had sent concerning the
arrowhead and the blowgun.

"He writes," Frank began, "that the South American
Indians who make this unusual type of arrowhead are

known to be dead shots. Also, that this is the first of its kind he's seen in the United States."

"No wonder Mr Scath couldn't identify it," Joe remarked.

"The blowgun used to shoot such a missile," the letter explained, "is a variety considerably shorter than the usual seven-foot one."

Joe grimaced. "That's why I got only a glimpse of it," he remarked. "It must have been small enough so that that fellow could hide it under his shirt when he started running into the woods. Read on, Frank."

"These blowguns," the letter continued, "are made by the South American Indians of either a hollow reed or a length of ironwood bored through with a red-hot iron. Blowguns have crude sights, which are sometimes made of animal teeth. And the blowers often succeed in sending missiles with great accuracy up to distances from fifty to sixty yards."

"The man who fired at me certainly was a crack shot," Joe commented.

"That's one fact," Mr Hardy observed, "which makes the Guatemalan connection a mystery. It's doubtful that a Central American could have used the blowgun with an accurate aim like that fellow had!"

Could it be possible, they wondered, that the enemies of the boys were not Guatemalans at all, but South American Indians or half-breeds of Spanish and Indian background?

Aunt Gertrude, who had been silent up to this point, now burst out, telling her nephews once again that she thought they should drop the case as quickly as possible.

"Why, Aunt Gertrude," Joe said, "we're just starting to get hot on this mystery."

"Don't worry," Frank assured her, "we have Dad around to keep us out of trouble."

Fenton Hardy smiled at this remark, then said, "I'm afraid that it's too late now, Gertrude. Even if the boys give up the case, which is unlikely"—and he chuckled—"their enemies would still keep after them."

The brothers agreed and Frank added, "We're going over to Tony's now."

At the Prito home Tony was taking in the morning mail from the box.

"Any news?" Joe asked him. "Any threats or missiles in your cereal this morning?"

Tony smiled, shaking his head. "Come on in," he said. "It's great that you've come over. I get pretty jittery over here wondering what's going to happen next."

"I'm afraid that our news is going to make you more jittery," Joe told him, as they all went into the living-room. He gave Tony the details of the burglary, the ambush, and the loss of the medallion. "Terribly sorry I muffed everything, Tony."

"Oh, that's okay. I guess what's on the medallion is the important part. And you say you memorized it. No wonder Valez wanted me to—"

Tony stopped speaking abruptly. The sudden crash of a windowpane had cut him short!

"Look!" Joe cried, staring at an arrowhead that had struck the wall and now lay on the rug. "It's exactly like the one that was fired at me!"

"And there's a note attached to this one, too!" Frank exclaimed as he picked up the object.

"What does it say?" Tony asked apprehensively. "Is it addressed to you or to me?"

"I'd guess it's meant for Joe and me," Frank replied. "The printing says 'Stop your detective work!' "

Joe, who had dashed out of the front door a moment after the missile struck, was standing on the porch when the other boys came running out to search for the person with the blowgun.

"We're too late," Joe said. "He's gone!"

"Wait a moment," Frank said. "Judging from the angle at which the shot came in here, the man must have aimed from the trees diagonally across the street."

Near the wooded area, a telephone lineman was at work on his truck. The boys hurried over to him and asked if he had seen a man with a blowgun.

"Blowgun?" The husky linesman laughed. "Are you fellows trying to kid me?"

"Well, did you see anyone near this area in the past few minutes?" Frank queried.

"Yes, come to think of it, I did," the phone man replied. "I saw a man cutting through the trees."

"What did he look like?" Frank asked eagerly.

"Short. A skinny guy with a black moustache."

Frank looked at Joe and Tony and the boys nodded to one another. This might be the same man who had fired the first missile! And possibly he was one of the men who had waylaid Joe on the road to the airport. But again the question of whether the man was Torres or Valez arose in the boys' minds.

"Thanks," Frank said to the linesman, and the trio returned to Tony's.

"Do you suppose Dad's hunch about Torres being in Bayport is right and he's a blowgun man too?" Joe observed, as they prepared to repair the broken window.

"Could be," said Tony, frowning with worry as he left for a nearby hardware store to buy a new pane of glass.

Tony, with the help of the Hardys, soon had the new pane in place. Then they sat down to plan further strategy in tracking down the owner of the blowgun.

"Maybe we ought to wear missile-proof suits if we're to continue looking!" joked Frank.

"Remember, we're to meet every half hour on the through street at the west end of the block we're searching," Frank reminded the others as they started off on their separate ways.

Three times the boys met as they had planned, without any report of success. Then, heading north, towards the poorer, more crowded sections near the electric company's power plant, Frank was startled to see a possible suspect approaching on the same side of the street. He was short, slender, and black-moustached. When Frank got a better look at the man, he was fairly sure that he was the one who had shot the arrowhead at Joe.

"If he's our man, I hope that he doesn't see me," Frank thought as he dodged into a shop entrance. "If he doesn't, I'll be able to find out where he's staying."

But in the same instant the man had evidently recognized Frank. Without a moment's hesitation, he whirled about and disappeared down a dingy apartment-house cellarway!

Frank dashed up the street after him. But just before reaching the apartment house he stopped. Had the man fled through the building? Or at this moment was he aiming one of the deadly missiles, ready to let it fly if Frank appeared?

· 12 · *The Matter of a Moustache*

REALIZING that he was exposed to the deadly aim of the blowgun marksman should he peer from the cellarway, Frank darted out of range behind a parked car. Ducking low to lessen the chance of being hit by the concealed enemy, he dashed across the street to take refuge in a doorway.

"Hey, Frank!" a familiar voice rang out as the young sleuth crouched, waiting for the moustached man's next move. "What are you doing—playing hide and seek?"

"Chet Morton!" Frank cried as his stout friend ambled across the street towards him. "Come over here. Hurry!"

As Chet joined Frank in the shadows of the doorway, he told him that he was on his way to buy some horse feed. Frank quickly related what had happened to him and asked Chet to run to police headquarters two blocks distant. "Tell them to rush a patrol car to 48 Weller Street!"

Without even a backward glance, Chet hurried away. Frank kept his eyes glued to the building entrance but saw no sign of the fugitive. Minutes passed. Grimly Frank thought, "Did Chet get to the police safely, or was he too ambushed?"

Then the welcome wail of the patrol siren sounded as the radio car streaked round the corner into view. As it pulled alongside, Frank dashed from his hiding place.

"The man's in there!" he cried to Sergeant Murphy, who was in charge of four policemen. They leaped from the car. As everyone ran towards the house, Frank described the suspect. "And be careful," he warned the officers. "He's got a deadly aim!"

"Cover the back entrance!" Murphy tersely commanded two of the officers. Instructing a third policeman to stay with Frank out front, he himself and the fourth man dashed into the building.

Several minutes later, as a small crowd was gathering to watch the action, Sergeant Murphy and the patrolman appeared on the sidewalk.

"Sorry, Frank," he said, "but we've found no trace of a black-moustached man. We checked every apartment. The superintendent tells me that no one in the building matches your description of the guy."

Murphy called back the other patrolmen. Frank, smarting with disappointment at their failure to capture the suspect, thanked the police for their effort. The officers pulled away.

"I'm still not satisfied that that blowgun guy is not in there," Frank told Chet. As they started towards the crosstown avenue, he stopped short and said excitedly, "I have an idea!"

"Tell me!" Chet said.

"We'll circle back round the block," Frank explained, "and approach the building from the other direction for a look."

Puffing, Chet kept up with Frank and the two quickly covered the distance round the block. They took up a position in a café from which they had a clear view of the apartment house.

"Do you really believe he's still in there?" Chet asked, munching on the third jam doughnut he had been unable to resist. "We've been here half an hour."

Without taking his eyes off the entrance, Frank replied, "If we wait long enough we may see him."

Ten more minutes passed. Frank began to think about his brother and Tony. They would be waiting at the crosstown avenue.

"Chet!" he suddenly gasped. "There he is now— what a break!" He pointed to a short, slender man leaving the front door of the building.

"But you said he had a moustache!" Chet exclaimed. "This man doesn't!"

"He must have shaved it off," Frank replied. "And he's also wearing a different suit. But there's no question in my mind that he's our boy!" Quickly Frank opened the café door and motioned for his friend to follow.

"What are we going to do?" Chet asked nervously.

"Trail him!" Frank replied in a low voice. "See, he thinks he's given us the slip. Hasn't even looked over his shoulder."

Keeping a safe distance behind, the boys followed the man as he strode jauntily down the block. They stopped when he entered a hardware store.

"Listen, Chet," Frank whispered. "He wouldn't recognize you. Drift over to the store and see what's going on."

Frank ducked behind a large tree as his pal followed instructions and appeared to be looking at the display in the store window. Soon Chet retraced his steps and hurried back excitedly.

"He's buying a window blind and some brackets!" he whispered, as a milk truck pulled up in front of the tree where the boys stood. "And I heard the clerk call him Mr Valez."

"Watch it!" warned Frank, equally excited, as he saw the man step outside the store. He glanced in both directions, not seeing the boys now concealed by the milk truck, then started back towards the apartment house.

Frank asked Chet to return to the store and see what he could learn about Valez from the clerk. "I'm going to follow him!" he said, still keeping his eyes glued on the man.

"Where shall I meet you?" Chet asked.

"On the corner of the crosstown avenue," his friend replied. "Explain to Joe and Tony if you arrive before I do."

They parted and Frank hurried after the stranger. As the man turned into the apartment entrance, he paused to open a mailbox, calmly inspected some letters, and disappeared into the foyer.

"He certainly seems to live here," thought Frank, wondering where the man had been when Sergeant Murphy had inspected the place. Then, having convinced himself that this was the base of operations for the enemy, Frank headed towards the avenue to join his friends.

"What happened to you?" Joe asked as Frank approached the corner.

"We've been waiting half an hour and nothing to report," said Tony. "How about you?"

Both boys listened wide-eyed to Frank's tale of discovering the suspect at the apartment house. His account was interrupted by the arrival of Chet.

"I'm afraid what I learned is of no help," he panted. "The clerk told me that the man's full name is Eduardo Valez. He's the superintendent of the building and has been for years. Another thing, he's never had a moustache and the clerk said Valez is well thought of in the neighbourhood."

"Guess I jumped to conclusions," said Frank. "But maybe there's a connection between the superintendent and the blowgun guy!"

"Could be!" Joe said thoughtfully. "Perhaps Eduardo wears a fake moustache as a disguise, or"—and his eyes brightened—"he may have a moustached twin who's the real villain!"

"That's a good solution!" exclaimed Tony. "The twin might have hidden in his brother's apartment while the police were searching the building."

Frank proposed that the quartet go to his home and talk over the mysterious twist of events with Mr Hardy. "Maybe Radley ought to cover the apartment house. I think we'd be recognized if our deductions are correct," he added.

"Sorry, fellows, but I promised to get back to the farm and pick apples," Chet said. "It's hard work, but it's safer than this detective business."

"Might not be if you eat too many apples," Joe quipped.

Tony declared that he would like nothing better than to continue work on the case, but he was due to drive a truck for the Prito Construction Company the rest of the afternoon. He accompanied Chet to the car park where he had left his jalopy.

The brothers went directly home and told Mr Hardy of their attempt to capture the assailant. Immediately their father called his assistant, Sam Radley, and asked him to watch the building.

"And now, to save time," the detective told the boys, "I'm going to check with the Immigration Service and learn what people named Valez have come into this country and where they are. Meanwhile, I want you both to go and question the building superintendent."

Eduardo Valez proved to be friendly. Through the speaking tube at the entrance he told the brothers to come to his basement apartment. It was very attractively furnished in mahogany and on a mantel stood several carved figures.

"Are these wooden pieces from your country?" Joe asked with interest. "They're beautiful!"

Without a moment's pause Mr Valez replied, "Yes, from Guatemala—my native land. They are made of the best grade of mahogany," he added proudly.

The Hardys were startled by the fact that this man was from Guatemala—some of the telltale ashes were of Central American mahogany! Frank decided to pursue the subject of a twin brother indirectly.

"You have relatives down there?" he asked casually.

"Ah, yes. Many." The man beamed. "But I'm—how you say—hundred per cent American these past five years," he replied in his soft Spanish accent.

"And relatives in this country?" Joe interrupted with a disarming smile. Valez did not reply at once and the youth realized that he was not being understood. "I mean, do you have, for instance, a brother in the United States?"

The man's pleasant manner was ruffled for a moment. He dropped his eyes and his jaw tightened. Recovering his composure, he smiled and said, "No, I have no brother in this country."

Both boys felt embarrassed, as if they had somehow hurt the man's feelings. The Hardys thanked Eduardo Valez for answering their questions and left.

"Another lead that led nowhere," Frank sighed, as

they headed back home. "You know, Joe, I sort of liked that guy. He seemed on the up-and-up."

Joe nodded and replied, "Well, Dad should have the data by now on other people named Valez."

When the boys entered their home, Mr Hardy called them into the living-room. "All the visas have been checked," he told them. "Each entry has been accounted for and in no way could be called a suspect. We can only conclude that your suspect is either a citizen or that he has entered this country illegally."

"I'll bet that he's here illegally," Joe remarked, and his father agreed.

"I think your man either jumped ship or was smuggled into this country across the border," Mr Hardy continued.

Just then, Mrs Hardy appeared and announced dinner. She had no trouble in getting the three male members of the family to the table.

"Smell the food!" Joe chirped. "That's one clue which isn't false."

After a delicious dinner of charcoal-broiled steak, corn on the cob, and ice-cream cake, the boys went into a huddle with their father on where to tackle their sleuthing next.

"I believe we ought to wait for a report from Sam Radley," Mr Hardy said. "Give yourselves a few hours' rest."

His sons took the advice and went to bed at nine o'clock. As they were dressing the next morning, Mrs Hardy called to say that they were wanted on the phone.

"It sounds like Chet Morton," she added.

Frank hurried to his mother's bedroom to answer on

the extension phone. "Hello," he said. "This is Frank
Hardy."

"F-Frank," a quaking voice began. It was Chet's.
"I've j-just got a letter with a warning in it. Even has
some ashes. The message says, 'You, too, are now
c-cursed!' "

·13· *A Near Capture*

"FRANK," Chet groaned over the phone, "when I
offered to help you fellows, I d-didn't bargain for this!"

Calming his friend, Frank said he was sorry and
advised Chet to stay close to the Morton farm. "Don't
risk any trips to Bayport by yourself," Frank continued. "If you have to go to town, make sure you
don't try it alone."

Chet promised. "You couldn't get me away, even if I
was offered a whole roast turkey to eat."

Just as Frank hung up, the morning post arrived.
A suspicious-looking envelope addressed to "Mr F.
Hardy and Sons" lay in the box when Joe opened it.
Quickly Joe slit the envelope which was postmarked
Bayport. It contained a quantity of ashes!

"Dad, come here quick!" he called. "You too,
Frank!"

When they reached the hallway, Joe began to read
the printed note. " 'We have sent warnings to your
friends Tony Prito and Chet Morton. This is the last
time we are warning you to stop your sleuthing in this
case or harm will come to you.' "

"No need to microtome these ashes!" Frank exclaimed, "Central American mahogany again!" He looked closely at one unburned bit of the familiar wood which he had picked out of the envelope.

Meanwhile, at the Morton farm, Chet's pretty, dark-haired sister Iola was worried about him. She had never seen him more nervous. And she too was upset over the note. Hoping to take her brother's mind off the threat, she proposed a steak roast that evening at the Elkin Amusement Park.

"We'll go early and have some fun."

Iola, who was usually Joe's date, soon extracted promises from Callie Shaw, the attractive blonde who often dated Frank, and two other girls, Maria Santos and Judy Rankin, to come along. Then she invited Tony and the Hardys.

"Swell idea!" agreed Joe, who answered the phone. "We haven't seen you girls for a long time. Seems like a hundred years."

"To us also," said Iola. "We've reserved fireplace Number Twelve for our picnic," she explained. "An attendant will watch our food and lay the fire for us."

"Sounds like a pretty soft assignment." Joe laughed. "We'll have nothing to do but eat the food."

"Oh, you'll have to do the barbecuing," Iola replied. "And of course we'll go on the rides in the amusement area and visit the Room of Horrors!"

"Just step in and look at Frank's and my room any time," Joe replied, "and you won't need to go to the one at the park."

"Well, you should feel right at home," Iola rejoined, chuckling.

She told him that Chet and Tony were coming. "But seriously, will you both be able to go with us too?"

"You bet. We'll pick up the other girls shortly after five," Joe replied.

"Meet us at the farm," Iola said. "We've fixed up something special. 'Bye now!"

About three o'clock Frank phoned Callie to tell her the plan. After a little conversation she said, "Frank, a funny thing happened here a short while ago. I didn't think anything about it at the time, but now it worries me."

"What is it?"

Callie said she felt that stupidly, but unwittingly, she had told a complete stranger about the picnic plans. A man had come to the Shaw's back door selling novel kitchen gadgets he carried in a small suitcase.

"I bought a couple of them," Callie went on. "Then suddenly the man said, 'You're a friend of Frank Hardy's, aren't you? Nice guy.'"

"I hope you agreed," Frank said teasingly.

Callie did not laugh. "I'm worried, Frank, because I told him about the picnic plans. He seemed so nice, but now I realize he asked me a lot of questions. Frank, he may be a spy—one of those men from the patriotic society Iola was telling me about."

Frank asked if the man spoke with a Spanish accent and had a moustache.

"No," Callie said.

"Then stop worrying," said Frank. "Just concentrate on having a good time."

Callie promised to do so, then Frank put down the phone. Despite his light-hearted attitude about the incident, he was alarmed. There was no question in his mind that the kitchen-gadget salesman was a phoney.

As Frank sat mulling it over, Aunt Gertrude and his

mother came through the hall. "A penny for your thoughts," Mrs Hardy said, smiling.

When Frank told them, Aunt Gertrude was alarmed. "You'd better decide on another picnic spot," she said firmly.

"What do you think, Mother?" Frank asked.

Mrs Hardy thought a moment, then said that if there were any change of plan the girls would have to know why. Then Iola would worry because of Chet's warning, and Callie would be embarrassed because she would feel she was to blame.

"It might be better if you boys just keep alert when you're at the park," she concluded.

Aunt Gertrude started to protest but changed her mind and left for the kitchen.

"After all," Mrs Hardy told Frank, "that salesman may have been an innocent person. But if he has any evil intentions, you boys will be safer at the amusement park—with so many people around—than at any other place." So no change in plans was made.

After picking up the three girls and Tony Prito in their father's car, the brothers set off for the Morton farm at five o'clock. When they arrived, the group learned that Chet had piled hay into his father's truck, so that they could all go together on an old-fashioned hayride to the amusement park.

"This is swell!" Joe exclaimed.

"We're all ready to go!" Chet announced. "Don't forget the food, Iola!"

Callie laughed. "As if you'd let us leave without it!" she teased.

"Len is going to drive us," Iola announced.

A big cheer went up from the boys who had been ready to flip a coin to see who would have to pass up sitting with the crowd to do the driving. Len Wharton, a good-natured former cowboy, had recently come to work on the Morton place.

Len grinned. "Shucks, I figured that if I was seventeen I sure wouldn't want to be stuck with the drivin'."

"Well, what are we waiting for?" Tony asked, and everyone climbed in.

All along the way the group sang. "We'll be hoarse before we get there," Callie said, laughing.

Zigzagging through the back lanes, Len stretched the short run to Elkin Park into an hour-long ride. As the picnickers got out, he said, "You jest call me at the farm when you want to git on back."

The baskets of food were carried to the reserved fireplace, where the attendant stored them away.

"How about taking in the amusements before we eat?" Joe suggested. "I guess you can wait, eh, Chet?"

"Sure." Chet laughed. "Let's go!"

For an hour the four couples whirled about on the thrill rides, took a boat down the chute-the-chutes, and laughed their way through the Fun House, where crazy mirrors made everyone take on all kinds of shapes.

"Look!" Chet roared. "In this mirror I'm skinny!"

"Better stand there until after supper," Tony retorted.

"And now—the best for last," Iola announced. "Before we go back to the fireplace, let's take a ride on the roller coaster."

Climbing into the first four seats of the bright red cars, the young people strapped themselves in. The motor rumbled into action and the caterpillarlike train of cars snaked along the track to start the steep climb to the first turn. As the cars rose higher and higher, the lights of the town flickered into view.

"Feel the wind!" Iola cried. "We're going to blow right out!"

The cars reached the summit and rolled smoothly round the bend. Suddenly they snapped into the steep dive! Maria and Judy screamed as the cars streaked past the white uprights. Hitting the bottom of the run, they plunged into the blackness of a short tunnel, and emerged on a level centre track that passed the entrance booth. As the coaster began another climb, Frank uttered a gasp.

"Joe!" he exclaimed to his brother in the seat behind. "He's there! Near the ticket booth!"

"Who?" Callie asked.

Not wanting to worry her, Frank merely said it was a man for whom he and Joe were looking. Through the rest of the breathtaking swoops and turns, the brothers could think of little else. The chances of spotting the blowgun suspect again in the crowd milling round the park were small. Nevertheless, they would try.

The instant the ride was over, Frank and Joe excused themselves and darted in and out of the crowd, but did not find the man.

"I'm sure that he has left the park," said Frank. "But this means he's still in Bayport. So our case isn't so hopeless after all."

When the boys reached fireplace Number Twelve, they found the picnic baskets placed on a redwood table. The attendant had laid the fire of kindling and charcoal. It was ready to light.

Stars twinkled in the night sky. "How about another song?" Tony suggested to the group.

A merry tune was started and the girls began to spread out the food. Chet knelt at the fireplace, struck a match, and set the fire. The flames, fanned by the stiff breeze, licked rapidly through the kindling. In a short time a fine blaze was roaring.

"When it dies down, we'll put on the steaks," Chef Chet announced.

Suddenly there came a terrific explosion from the fireplace! Chet fell backwards several feet from the flames as glowing embers rained down on the entire group.

•14• *The Black Sheep*

"HELP!" cried Iola frantically. "My hair's on fire!" Desperately she beat her palms against her head, screaming in terror.

Ripping off his jacket, Frank flung it about her head, snuffing out the flame that endangered the frightened girl. Leading her away from the roaring fireplace, he said reassuringly, "You're okay now. Some of your hair's singed a bit, but it gives you that carefree look!" he added lightly to calm her.

Iola, though still shaky, managed a laugh. "It's one way of getting a new hair style," she replied gamely. "And thanks for the rescue."

Chet declared he was all right—aside from having the breath knocked out of him by his fall. The scare over, they all tried to figure out what had caused the blast. Had some explosive substance been sprayed on the kindling? Or had someone planted a crude bomb in the fireplace?

"If the latter is true," Frank thought, "then the salesman at Callie's *was* a spy!"

The girl ran to his side. "I told you! I'm the cause of this!" She quickly repeated her story of the salesman to the others.

"Did you mention fireplace Number Twelve to the man?" Frank asked.

"Yes, I did. Oh, dear!"

Frank put a hand on her shoulder. "Callie, no real harm has been done, so forget it," he said soothingly.

A crowd quickly gathered and began to ask questions. Several wondered if it would be safe for them to use another fireplace.

"Where's the attendant?" Joe called out.

The worried, grey-haired man who had been laying another fire hurried over. Joe questioned him. "I didn't put anything but wood and paper in the fireplace," he said nervously.

"Was anyone near this spot while we were away?" Joe asked him quietly.

The attendant scratched his head, then said a man with a moustache had offered to help him lay the fire in Number Twelve. "I told him I'd do it myself," the man continued. "He did hang around, though."

The Hardys did not voice aloud the suspicion that the salesman had told Torres or Valez the picnic plans. They merely assured the attendant that he was not to blame. The girls found another fireplace, and Chet and Tony carried the baskets over to it.

"Joe," said Frank, "we'd better search the embers in Number Twelve. We might find a clue."

"Right."

Sprinkling a can of water over the still-burning wood, they raked through the damp remains for evidence.

"Here's something," Joe whispered. He handed Frank one of the mysterious arrowhead missiles! "This explains a lot. The arrowhead was intended for one of us!"

"We were sure lucky," Frank said grimly.

"Something went wrong with the way that fellow had the charge rigged up," Joe suggested. "Let's see if we can find out what." Carefully the boys continued examining the embers.

"Guess this is it," Frank said, pulling out a small metal container. "This homemade bomb had the charge and the missile in it."

"The bottom of the container melted and the arrowhead fell out before the charge went off," Joe continued, "which kept the missile from shooting out."

"Hey, what's this?" Frank said excitedly as he reached into the ashes and pulled out a window-blind bracket. "This must have been part of what triggered the bomb. Say, didn't Chet tell us that Valez, the superintendent, bought some brackets at the hardware store?"

"Exactly," Joe replied. "There's no doubt about it in my mind now. That man's mixed up in the case."

"It's strange, too," Frank added, "because he seemed to be a very nice person, not the kind who'd plant deadly explosives."

The boys decided that they would say nothing about their find, but the next morning would investigate Eduardo Valez again. Together, the brothers joined the other young people. Try as they might, the group found little pleasure in the meal, though the food was delicious. The shock of the explosion and the narrow escape of Chet and Iola had caused them all to lose their appetites.

"Even I don't feel hungry," Chet lamented. "We should have eaten on the way out here."

Iola asked Frank to phone Len to come and get them. "At least," Frank said, smiling, "we had fun here before the explosion."

Early the following day, Mr Hardy and his sons drove across town to the apartment house for the purpose of questioning Valez.

"Good morning," the superintendent said affably as the boys introduced their father. "Come right in."

"We have no time for anything but the truth," Mr Hardy said firmly as he entered the apartment.

"Wh-why what do you mean?" the man replied. "I have not held back anything from your sons."

The detective told in detail the happenings at the amusement park. As he unfolded the account of the explosion and the narrow escape of the young people, Valez's face suddenly whitened. The superintendent raised his hand to stop Mr Hardy's recital. A look of distress came over the man's face and his mouth twitched as he prepared to speak.

"I—I am not the man you are searching for," he began slowly. Looking at Joe and Frank, he said, "I am sorry I did not tell you the truth at first. Now I will explain."

"Thank you," Mr Hardy said. "Go ahead."

"The man with the black moustache," Mr Valez continued with a pained expression, "he is my brother. He is the—what you call—black sheep of our family. Six of us children and he is the only one to break the law."

"What is his name?" Mr Hardy asked.

"Luis."

"Where is he now?" Frank asked.

"I do not know, but he was staying with me for a short time."

"Which explains the moustache mystery," Joe remarked to Frank.

"Luis sneaked into this country," Valez went on. "He promised me the day before yesterday he would return to Guatemala at once, so I did not turn him over to the authorities when they came here asking about a moustached man. Luis left here while I was on an errand at the hardware store."

"Buying brackets," Joe said, half under his breath.

"Did you say something about brackets?" Valez asked quickly.

"We found a bracket in the remains of the fire," Joe replied.

"That is why I went to the hardware store," Mr Valez added. "There was a bracket missing from one of my apartments. So I went to buy another. And I purchased a new blind while I was there."

The superintendent went on to tell Mr Hardy and the boys that he was astonished to learn that his brother had become a suspect in a case of violence. "I thought Luis had come to the United States to get away from some little trouble at home. He said it blew over, so he was going back. Always I have defended my baby brother," said Eduardo, clenching his fists, "but now I see I can no longer do this."

"Is there anything else you think we should know?" Mr Hardy asked.

"Maybe this is not important," Valez replied, "but a couple of small mahogany objects disappeared, too. Luis might have them with him."

The Hardys quizzed the superintendent about the possibility of a connection between mahogany and any

Guatemalan superstitions. Valez explained that among certain people in Central America there was one such superstition, adding, "It's said if a person sends the ashes of a piece of native mahogany to his enemy, that man will be rendered powerless to harm the sender!"

Frank frowned. "That's a very strange idea."

Valez could give the Hardys no further help, so the detective and his sons thanked the superintendent and left. On the sidewalk, Frank and Joe speculated on the mysterious piles of warning embers and ashes.

"Luis must have burned some of his brother's mahogany pieces," Frank stated.

"But why the chicken bones?" asked Joe. "Unless," he added thoughtfully, "he didn't have any of Eduardo's wood handy at the time. He probably figured we wouldn't know the difference."

On the corner, where Mr Hardy had parked his car, the trio met Sam Radley. The assistant reported that the moustached man had not been back to the apartment while either he or his relief man was on duty.

When the Hardys returned home, Aunt Gertrude told the boys that Tony Prito had called. He had said Mr Scath had asked him to take away the part of the inheritance which the museum was unable to use.

"And he wants you to go over there with him this evening," Aunt Gertrude concluded.

Shortly after supper, Frank and Joe drove off in the convertible to Tony's. There, they transferred to Mr Prito's small pickup truck.

"Let's drive out and get Chet," Joe said. "I'll bet he's just sitting around still worrying about the threat he received. Maybe he'd enjoy helping us."

The others grinned and Tony said, "You know how he loves work—not at all!"

Chet was reading a magazine when the trio arrived. At the boys' suggestion that he go along, he puckered his lips. "I don't know about taking a chance on tangling with a bombmaker," he said, "especially in that weird museum."

"Aw, come on—be a sport!" Frank urged.

Chet was finally persuaded to join the group and they drove off. The museum had closed for the evening by the time the boys arrived. While Mr Scath showed Tony what he wanted removed, mostly small articles, the Hardys and Chet wandered about the various rooms, now only dimly lit.

At the South American display Frank and Joe noticed that Mr Scath had arranged the shrunken heads on a ledge. The temptation to have some fun with Chet, who was still in the adjoining gallery, was too much for Joe to resist. Gingerly fastening one of the grotesque heads to a window pole, he hid behind a column near the door and called Chet.

"Coming!" his unsuspecting friend replied.

As his footsteps grew louder, Joe stuck the pole farther and farther out and began to swing it gently from side to side. The head, dangling by its glossy black hair, looked ghastly in the dimmed lights.

"*Ee-eee!*" Chet croaked and stopped dead. "Frank! Joe! Where are you?" The startled boy turned and fled back to the other gallery.

Joe quickly restored the head to its place in the exhibit and called Chet again, asking what was wrong. By then, Chet had realized that a prank was being played on him and sheepishly he returned to the room.

The appearance of Tony took Chet's mind off the joke. Mr Scath had finished showing him what he was to take away and given Tony a key. He suggested that the four boys go to the storage shed at the rear of the museum grounds for some crates and pack the articles in them.

"We'll carry the things back to my place," Tony explained, "and put them in the cellar."

As the boys went out of the rear door he handed the key to Chet, who was the last one out. The four youths crossed the dark yard, and entered the shed. A stack of various-sized crates was piled near the door.

Suddenly Joe put his finger to his lips. "Sh-h!" he warned.

The boys stopped short. A faint cry had sounded from the museum.

"Help!" It sounded like Mr Scath's voice.

"H-help!" The cry died out.

· 15 · *Hunting an Assailant*

DROPPING the crates, the boys ran to answer Mr Scath's call for help. After the two outcries, they had heard nothing more.

"I don't see how anyone could have broken in," Frank said.

"I'm afraid it's my fault," Chet admitted as they reached the rear entrance. "I didn't lock this door—thought we'd be right back."

Frank turned the knob and they hurried inside. Chet locked the door.

"Be careful of a sniper!" Frank warned the others. "And keep together!"

The curator was not in sight and when Frank called

he did not answer. The boys rushed to Mr Scath's office, but he was not in it.

"Mr Scath must be on the side of the building nearest the shed," Joe suggested. "His voice wouldn't have carried from the other sections."

He led the way into the Egyptian Room and switched on the lights. Mr Scath was sprawled on the floor, unconscious! The boys rushed over.

"There's blood on his face!" Tony exclaimed. "He's been slugged."

"And look at his pockets!" Frank cried. "They've been pulled inside out."

"Oh, if I had only locked the door!" Chet wailed, feeling he was responsible.

"Don't worry about that now," Frank replied. "Joe, you and Tony search the building for the slugger, while Chet and I attend to Mr Scath."

Joe and Tony headed for the opposite end of the museum, and Frank and Chet knelt beside the injured man and inspected the head wound. Fortunately, it was not deep and the curator's colour was returning to normal. A moment later Mr Scath gave a low moan and his eyes flickered open.

"Help me up," he said feebly, trying to rise.

"Lie still," Frank urged. "Don't try to move."

He recalled having seen a first-aid kit on an open shelf in the curator's office and asked Chet to get it.

Anxious to make amends for his carelessness, the stout youth hurried off. A whiff of spirits of ammonia revived Mr Scath. Frank gently swabbed away the blood. Luckily the man had been struck only a glancing blow.

"Feeling better?" he asked.

"My head feels clearer," Mr Scath replied. He sat up with Chet's assistance.

"Here, let me put a patch over that cut," Frank said. When this was done, the boys helped the curator to his feet and back to his office.

"What happened?" Frank asked, after Mr Scath had seated himself in a comfortable chair.

"I was in here alone, waiting for you fellows, when I heard a noise in the Egyptian Room. I went to investigate."

"Did you see someone?" Chet asked.

"Yes. There was a masked man standing alongside the first big column. He demanded that I hand over the Texichapi medallion from Tony's collection."

"Yes?" Frank said eagerly as the man paused.

"I told him that I had no idea what he was talking about," Mr Scath continued. "Then he pulled out a blackjack and threatened me. I got a bit flustered—tried to fight him off—and I shouted a couple of times, hoping you'd hear me. Then he struck me and I blacked out!"

"What was his build?" Frank asked.

"Short, thin. Had black hair."

Frank whistled. "The blowgun man or Torres," he told Mr Scath.

"If it was Luis Valez," Chet exclaimed, "then he didn't go back to Guatemala after all!"

Frank nodded. He asked permission to use Mr Scath's phone, then called Chief Collig and told him about the attack.

"Hold the fort!" the chief responded. "We'll be right there!"

Meanwhile, Joe and Tony had searched the entire north section of the museum without finding the curator's attacker. The boys went back to join the others in the Egyptian Room.

Not finding them there, they decided that their friends must have led Mr Scath back to his office. As they were about to check there, Joe suddenly noticed something on the floor. He hurried over to pick it up. "Tony!" he exclaimed. "This is a Guatemalan coin!"

Joe and Tony hurried to the office and showed the coin to the others. Mr Scath said that it was not a coin from the museum's collection. It was highly probable that his assailant had lost it.

"Let's check Tony's curios," Joe suggested. "If the intruder was Valez, that's what he was after."

They hurried to the gallery containing the old musical instruments and the jewellery. As the ceiling light was turned on, everyone gasped. The glass had been neatly removed from one of the cases. Every ring, bracelet, and necklace was gone!

"Oh, oh!" Mr Scath cried. He wobbled unsteadily and Frank helped him to a marble bench.

At this moment a siren sounded at the front entrance and the night bell rang insistently.

"It's the police," Chet announced.

"Take my key," Mr Scath said to Frank. "Let them in."

Chief Collig strode in with two other officers. Quickly they were told about the attack and theft, and started a thorough search of the building. But it was soon ascertained that the attacker had escaped. Chief Collig said, "From now on we'll keep a guard here on a twenty four-hour basis. Sampson, you stay here right now. I'll send out a teletype on the missing jewels and a description of the intruder."

Mr Scath handed a spare key to Sampson, then said

to the boys, "Come back another time and pick up the curios." Everyone but the officer on duty left.

The next morning Frank and Joe decided to question Eduardo Valez again, hoping he might have heard from his brother. They set out very early for the apartment house.

"My brother?" the man replied to Frank's query. "No, I have not seen or heard of him since you called with your father."

"Did Luis ever tell you the exact nature of the trouble he had in his country?" Frank asked.

"Not really," the superintendent replied. "He did say something about an argument over a buried treasure, but Luis is such a braggart I paid little attention."

"Buried treasure!" Frank exclaimed. "Did he ever say anything about medallions?"

"Medallions?" Eduardo Valez mused. "No, he never did. Oh, I am so sad about the whole affair."

The boys left, feeling sorry for him.

"I think that we ought to spend the rest of this day making an intensive search of Tony's curios for that Texichapi medallion," Joe proposed. "I believe that's what Luis was hunting for when Mr Scath discovered him. So maybe we've overlooked some hiding place where Tony's uncle put it."

"We'll get Tony and Chet," Frank answered. "And, after all, we haven't taken those curios from the museum which the curator didn't want."

At two o'clock they all met at the museum. Mr Scath, still wearing a bandage on his forehead, smiled as the boys started off to the shed for the crates. "I hope we have better luck today!" he said.

The boys brought the crates to the basement and went to work. As each curio was examined closely, those to be taken by Tony were placed in a crate. The others were returned to the shelves. An hour passed. One crate had already been filled but they had not found the medallion.

Chet Morton, still upset over leaving the museum door unlocked the night before, had worked hard, trying to make amends.

At the moment he was fingering a solid mahogany, highly polished ball.

Picking it up, he removed a foil wrapping that covered part of the surface. His sharp eyes detected a thin, almost invisible line that went completely round the circumference of the ball. In his excitement to get a closer view of it, the ball slipped out of his grasp. It hit the cement and rolled across the floor, past the packed crates.

"Playing games?" Joe teased.

"I'm sorry," Chet groaned, going after the ball. "I wasn't playing. I—"

He interrupted himself as he stooped to pick up the ball. It had started to come apart at the seam. A strip of rich blue velvet showed in the opening. Inside he saw the brilliant glint of metal!

Prising apart the two sections, he cried out, "Fellows, come here quick!"

·16· *News of Buried Treasure*

"THE second medallion!" Chet exclaimed gleefully. "Fellows, I've found the second medallion!"

Gleaming in the light, on its velvet bed inside the

mahogany ball, lay the medallion. Carefully Frank lifted it from the hollow into which it had been wedged and held it for the others to see.

"There's the clue that Wortman gave us!" he said. "See the word *Texichapi*!"

"And there are strange engraved lines similar to the ones on the stolen medallion," Joe added.

Frank slipped the medallion back into the ball. "I'd like to show this to Dad and examine it very carefully," he said.

"It's okay with me," Tony answered. "But after what happened to Joe with the first medallion, watch your step."

The crates of less valuable objects were taken to the Prito home, then the Hardys sought out their father. To insure complete privacy from eavesdroppers, the trio went to the garage laboratory. There they examined the ball and the medallion. The Hardys concluded that the ball had been designed originally as a secret place to hold small pieces of valuable jewellery.

The boys wrote down from memory the pattern of lines on the stolen coin, then traced the new ones. By comparing markings, the three detectives concluded that the lines from the two coins, when superimposed, did seem to indicate a detailed map.

"It must show the area near the treasure that Luis Valez is looking for," Frank remarked.

"And the opal probably marks the spot where the treasure is hidden," Joe added. "I'm sure it isn't placed on the medallion just for decoration. Boy, I'd like to find that spot myself!"

"But it's in Texichapi—the land of nowhere," Frank reminded him.

"Let's hope we can learn what country Texichapi is

in," said Mr Hardy. "Meanwhile, you boys had better memorize these lines on the medallion and then we'll place it in my safe."

Frank and Joe drew the markings which were on the medallion again and again until they could do them perfectly from memory. Then the papers were burned so that nothing was left for anyone to steal.

"I wonder," mused Mr Hardy, "whether your friend Willie knew the value of both medallions. This one feels like solid gold to me and it certainly has the same lustre as a gold piece. Maybe Willie was just acting dumb because he feared Tony might refuse to sell him the coins once they were located." His sons said that they wished they knew.

The medallion was locked in Mr Hardy's file-safe. Then the boys and their father sat down in his study and continued to discuss the mystery.

"I know that you've consulted all kinds of maps to locate a place called Texichapi," Mr Hardy said, "but I'm going to make another try to find out where it is." He reached for the phone.

Being personally acquainted with various Central and South American consulates, the detective called them one by one and inquired about the place name. None of the men had ever heard of it.

Later in the evening, Mrs Hardy, who had come in with some crocheting, put it down and said, "Fenton, why don't you phone my friend Mrs Putnam? Her husband Roy has just come back from an expedition."

"The Central American explorer?" Mr Hardy asked. "Why, that's a great idea. But it's much too late to call anyone now."

"Not Roy Putnam," Mrs Hardy answered. "He

stays up half the night reading. I'll get him on the line for you."

Mr Putnam answered promptly and Mrs Hardy turned the phone over to her husband. The explorer became so interested in a brief account of the mystery that he offered to drive over at once.

"Be there about midnight," he promised.

The family went down to the living-room to await him. A thunderstorm came up shortly, necessitating the closing of all windows in the house except one near where they were seated. The wind whipped up sharply, banging a shutter on the east side of the house. Frank went to fasten it.

At five minutes before midnight the doorbell rang. Frank opened the door. The explorer, about fifty years old, and a man of commanding figure, removed his raincoat and shook hands with everyone.

"It's about time we got together." He smiled. "I've often heard my wife speak about this fine family."

"But you're so rarely at home," Mrs Hardy replied.

"That's right." The explorer smiled. "I've just returned from Guatemala, as a matter of fact."

"I'm sure then," Mr Hardy said, as his sons' eyes opened wide, "that you can give us a lot of help. Did you ever hear of Texichapi?"

A bolt of lightning flashed, startling them all. Then Mr Putnam said, "When you mentioned Texichapi a moment ago, I was astounded. I never dreamed that anyone way up here would have any knowledge of that place."

"Where is it?" Frank questioned eagerly.

"Well, first of all," Mr Putnam began, "have you ever visited Guatemala?"

The Hardys said they had not.

"As you know," Mr Putnam began, "the country stretches from the Pacific to the Atlantic, just below Mexico. It's a rugged land—full of canyons, towering mountain ranges, and volcanoes.

"It's mostly Indian in population, and has some wonderful ruins. You come upon marvellous stone temples with walls completely carved in rare designs. Even out in the deepest jungle, in the most unsuspected places, one hears about buried temples and palaces."

A crash of thunder made it difficult to hear the explorer for a moment. Through the open window the sound of the driving downpour made an effective background for Mr Putnam's story.

"Guatemala has beautiful cities," he continued. "Beautiful colour splashed everywhere—cobbled streets in the old city sections, bright red roofs, light-blue and white walled houses, tropical flowers—parks full of them."

"Now how about Texichapi?" Mr Hardy asked mildly.

"Oh, yes." Mr Putnam smiled a bit sheepishly.

The boys moved closer to Mr Putnam and listened intently.

"Texichapi," the explorer began, "is a name given by a small tribe of Indians, the Kulkuls, to a mysterious and perhaps even mythical area many miles from Guatemala City."

"Do you mean it's possible that Texichapi really does exist?" Joe asked.

"Oh, there's a place that the Kulkuls call Texichapi," Mr Putnam replied. "I've heard various rumours about the region. The main one, I'd say, concerns a great treasure buried there," the explorer went

on, and the boys jumped in amazement. "Though I have many times tried to find out more about Texichapi, the Indians are very close-mouthed. Despite the legends surrounding the whole thing, I feel there may really be such a treasure."

"What makes you think so?" Mr Hardy asked.

Mr Putnam smiled. "Nothing definite," he replied. "Let's call it my explorer's hunch. It's not inconceivable that the Kulkul tribe guards the secret to Texichapi."

Joe's eyes glistened. "Boy, would I like to look for that treasure!"

Aunt Gertrude spoke up for the first time and snapped. "Why, those Indians might kill you if they found you looking for their treasure!"

Mr Putnam smiled tolerantly. "The Indians in Guatemala would not do that. The boys wouldn't have any trouble with them, but I also doubt that they would receive any clues about the treasure. No, you're more likely to have trouble with an occasional band of hostile, renegade Ladinos who have fled to the mountain regions.

"Ladinos," the explorer explained, "are Spanish-speaking, mixed-breed people. They are very proud and do no manual work like labouring in the fields or carrying loads. Mainly, they own stores and cantinas in the towns and villages and hold political offices."

Mr Hardy nodded thoughtfully, then said, "Mr Putnam, do you know whether any Guatemalans have a secret society that was organized to uncover this treasure or any other in the interests of their government?"

"Yes," Mr Putnam replied. "The only trouble is I don't know just which society you mean. They come and go—pop up all of a sudden, make a big noise, and disappear as quickly as they were formed."

The explorer went on to say that he had heard of no such group lately but he could find out. "If you'll allow me to use your phone," he said, "I'll call a friend of mine in Guatemala City whose business it is to investigate such groups. He'll know if there's any such organization operating now."

"Please do so," Mr Hardy said, showing the visitor to the hall phone.

"They won't mind my calling at this time of night." Mr Putnam grinned good-naturedly. "It's three hours earlier there."

The Hardys returned to the living-room while Mr Putnam put through his call. Several minutes passed before the man came back.

"My friend Soldo, who works for a government agency, tells me that there are rumours of another so-called patriotic society forming right now," Mr Putnam reported as he sat down. "His agency would welcome any information about it. If anything subversive is going on, he says, there'd be a good chance of nipping the plans in the bud."

The Hardys noticed that Mr Putnam had suddenly slumped in his chair, giving a tremendous yawn. Almost at the same moment, Frank and Joe themselves began to experience a queer lethargy. The boys sensed dimly that this was not a natural sleepiness!

Their father, too, felt himself growing drowsy. With a great effort, he tried to speak to the boys, but at this moment both his sons and Mr Putnam slipped from their chairs to the floor, unconscious. Fighting to remain awake, the detective got to his feet and moved across the room to assist his already sleeping wife and sister. But before he could reach them, he stumbled and blacked out!

·17· *A Ruse Works*

As the storm raged, the Hardy family and their guest remained in a deep stupor on the living-room floor. For twenty minutes none of the silent forms moved. Then the wind shifted, and the rain started pelting through the open window into the room.

Frank, lying nearest the window, was within range of the cold rain that was blowing in. Its continual spray across his upturned face gradually aroused him. Fighting desperately against the drowsiness that still engulfed him, the boy struggled to sit up. He looked dazedly around.

"They're all asleep!" he thought. "At least I hope it's just sleep."

Fearful, he spent the next few moments stumbling from one to another, feeling for pulses. All were alive! He wondered what had happened to cause this weird scene. Suddenly an answer came to Frank.

"Sleeping gas," he decided. "Where did it come from, though?"

Reviving a little more, Frank went to close the window against the storm. As he did so, he noticed the screening had been cut from its frame and lay on the floor. There was a slit in the centre of the wire mesh. Near it were several punctured, greenish pellets the size of a golf ball.

As he picked one up and examined it, Frank mused,

"These are gas pellets and must have been tossed in here."

He decided that the noise of the storm and the family's rapt interest in Mr Putnam's story would have prevented their noticing any sound at the window.

His legs steady now, Frank went to his mother's side, patted her face gently, and chafed her wrists. A few moments later Mrs Hardy's eyelids started to flutter open. Frank heard Mr Putnam talking indistinctly, but saw that he had not returned to consciousness.

"That's what happens to some people under the influence of gas," the boy thought.

The rest of the family began stirring. Frank, sensing that the danger of any lasting effect had passed, turned his thoughts in another direction. Who had hurled the pellets? Suddenly he remembered the screening on the floor. Had the person who threw the pellets in through the slit in the screen, then removed it while they were all unconscious and climbed into the house?

As if in answer to his unspoken query, Frank saw a masked man coming down the stairs! The intruder, apparently startled by Frank's unexpectedly quick recovery, jumped over the remaining steps and dashed for the front door.

Frank made a flying leap into the hall, realizing that here was an enemy who would spare no one to get what he wanted. Before the intruder could turn the doorknob, Frank crashed into him, sending the man sprawling on the hall floor.

Catlike, the masked man leaped to his feet and flailed out at Frank with both fists. One blow caught the boy on the cheekbone and split the skin. Enraged by this, Frank hurled himself in a fierce flying tackle at the man and knocked him against the steps!

While the fight was going on, Joe had regained consciousness. He stood up unsteadily and now glanced around. Out of the corner of his eye he saw the struggle and staggered to the hall. He was just in time to see Frank leap back as the man rolled off the stairs.

Frank, momentarily dazed by the impact of his tackle, raised both fists as his adversary scrambled to his feet pulling a blackjack from his pocket.

"No, you don't!" Joe roared. He leaped forward and swung a left uppercut to the man's chin that sent him to the floor.

Both boys jumped the intruder, stripped him of his blackjack, and pulled off his mask. The blowgun suspect!

"You're Luis Valez!" Frank accused him.

"No, that is not my name."

"Then what is it?" Joe demanded.

"I—I am not Valez," the suspect replied. "You have made a big mistake. I insist you let me go."

"You're in no position to insist on anything!" Frank replied harshly. "Breaking in here after having attempted to injure our whole family, you expect us to let you go! What do you take us for?"

"I have done nothing bad," the stranger insisted. "I have come into the wrong house."

Joe exploded. "You sure have! Now get up on your feet!"

Holding the man in a tight grip, the boys searched him quickly. Frank located a gas pellet in one of their prisoner's jacket pockets. In another, Joe felt something smooth and hard. He pulled it out. The Texichapi medallion!

"You still claim you entered the wrong house!"

Frank said in a steely voice. "How did you get into the file-safe?"

The man admitted hacking it with a hatchet which he had left upstairs. Then he refused to answer any more questions, though his eyes remained glued on the medallion Joe still held.

Frank, recalling that the gas pellets sometimes make a victim talk, decided to use a ruse to make Valez confess! Pretending to tear open the end of the one he had found, he said in a firm voice:

"This'll make you talk!"

The ruse worked. "Don't do that!" the man cried, terrified. "I will tell everything!"

By now, the others in the living-room had recovered from their enforced sleep. They expressed amazement that Frank had caught the burglar. Frank smiled, then said to the man, "Now tell your story."

"You are right," the stranger began slowly. "I am Luis Valez from Guatemala. But please, do not arrest my brother Eduardo. He knows nothing of what I do."

"And what *are* you doing?" Mr Hardy asked.

"I cannot tell you. All I want is to be shipped back to Guatemala."

"How can you go back without this medallion?" Joe asked, holding it up. "You wouldn't be very popular if you came back empty-handed."

The man hung his head and Frank demanded to know who had sent him to steal the coin. The dejected Guatemalan admitted that it was Torres, head of a patriotic society of which he was a member.

"We are searching for the treasure of Texichapi," he said quietly. "That is why we wanted this medallion."

"And why you stole the matching medallion," Joe said.

Valez denied this.

"How do we know you're not just part of a gang that's planning to keep this treasure for itself and not give it to your country?" Mr Hardy asked. "You've got a great deal of explaining to do. The police will want to hear it."

Frank went to the phone and called headquarters. "We didn't have to go chasing the blowgun man this time," he told the lieutenant on duty. "Caught him right in our home. He's the one who fired at Joe."

As Frank hung up, Valez protested vigorously that he had never seen Joe before tonight. In spite of the Hardy's accusations, the man stuck to his story. He admitted trying to buy Tony's curios, but denied having sent any threats or knowing anything about the stolen scimitar, the ashes, the museum theft, or the explosion in the picnic fireplace. He became sullen and seated himself on the steps, staring at the floor.

Mr Putnam, who until this moment had been looking on, got up and approached Frank and Joe. "Good work, boys!" the explorer praised them. "By the way, my friend in Guatemala will be glad to help you at any time. And now I think I'd better get home."

The Hardy family thanked him for coming and for the information he had given them.

"Just call me any time," Mr Putnam said as he started for the door. Then he smiled. "But next time ask your other guests to leave their sleeping gas at home!"

When Mr Hardy returned from escorting Mr Putnam to his car, he said, "It's too bad Willie Wortman isn't here too. He probably could give us some valuable information about Valez." The detective winked at his sons.

At the sound of the sailor's name, the prisoner leaped up from his chair. "Willie Wortman!" he exclaimed. "What do you know about him?"

"Plenty," Joe said noncommittally.

"How you know him?"

"Willie paid us a visit," Frank replied, "and told us about the medallions."

The Guatemalan's face went white with fear. He clenched his fists and made a break for the door but was promptly stopped by the boys.

"Valez, what do *you* know about Wortman?" Mr Hardy asked.

Assuming that the red-haired seaman had revealed more than he actually had, the prisoner admitted having met Wortman in a Guatemalan seaport.

"That sailor!" Valez snorted in disgust. "I fix him! He talk too much!"

When Valez had cooled down a little, Frank asked him where Wortman was at the moment.

"I don't know," Valez replied. "I have not seen him for a long time."

"It'll go easier with you if you tell the truth," Mr Hardy told him.

Valez shook his head determinedly. "I know nothing of things like that. I just want to go home to Guatemala."

The Hardys decided that there was little use in trying to question the man further. After sitting in a jail for a while, he might change his mind.

"Here come the police!" Joe said as a car pulled to a stop in the Hardy driveway.

Before leading Valez away, Chief Collig informed the Hardys that the stolen museum jewellery, including the scimitar, had been located in various pawnshops round the state. All of the proprietors described the seller as a dark-haired and moustached man who spoke with a Spanish accent. He had given his name as Romano.

Still protesting that he was innocent, Valez was handcuffed and led through the downpour by two officers to the waiting car.

·18· *A Helpful Confession*

THE next morning a surprise awaited Frank and Joe when they met their father at the breakfast table.

"Boys," he said, "I'll stake you to a trip to Guatemala —that is, if you want to go."

"Wow! Do we want to go!" Joe exclaimed, and Frank beamed.

The detective said he felt that they had come to an impasse in the solving of the mystery from the Bayport end. Furthermore, if an unscrupulous group was after the ancient treasure, the Guatemalan government would no doubt appreciate having it located by honest people.

"So we have two assignments," Frank said. "To keep the treasure from being stolen, and to locate it ourselves."

Mr Hardy nodded. "I'd like nothing better than to go with you, but since I'm on an important government case, I can't leave the country. I would like you to have company, though. How about Tony and Chet?"

"Bet you couldn't keep Tony home," said Joe. "About Chet, I don't know. He may be needed on the farm."

"Let's find out," Frank urged, and went to the phone.

Both Tony and Chet were flabbergasted to hear about all that had transpired at the Hardy home in the space of a few hours. And the idea of a trip intrigued them, though Chet began worrying about what kind of food he would have to eat in Central America. Mr Prito and Mr Morton gave permission for their sons to go.

Returning to Joe and his father, Frank reported the good news and said, "I'll call the airline office now for reservations." He did this, giving all the necessary data.

The following afternoon the four boys met and drove to the airfield, expecting to pick up their tickets for a flight early the next morning.

On the way Tony gave them some news of his inheritance. "Mr Scath called me a while ago," he said. "He has made an estimate of the total value of the curios I took home. If I can sell them for what he thinks they're worth, I'll have a nice sum of money."

"That's great," said Frank, and the other boys added their congratulations.

"Boy, I never dreamed that getting a shipment of curios would send us to Central America on a treasure hunt!" Tony exclaimed gleefully.

"I'm keen about going," Chet added, "but the idea of riding in those mountains and canyons on a mule sort of worries me."

"Maybe you can rent a water buffalo," Joe teased.

When the boys walked up to the clerk with whom

Frank had talked and gave their names, the man's face took on a disturbed look.

"Frank and Joe Hardy and Tony Prito have been cleared," he said, "but Chet Morton is not allowed to leave the country. I'm sorry, but he has been refused a permit."

"W-what?" Chet burst out, stunned by the news.

Joe demanded to know why their friend had been turned down.

"I don't know," the clerk replied, "but it must be a serious charge."

"Charge?" Chet gulped. "I haven't done any-thing!"

"This is the craziest thing I ever heard!" Joe stormed. "Someone has made a mistake."

The clerk explained that the manager of the office had told him about the Hardys being detectives. "Why don't you fellows do some investigating?" he suggested. "Unless your friend is cleared, he just won't be allowed to make the trip with you."

Frank asked for the card with the information on Chet Morton. The clerk passed it to him. It read simply: *Chester Morton, Bayport—request denied. Under restriction.*

"I wish you luck," the clerk said. "Your friend certainly doesn't look like the kind of a fellow who'd be in trouble with the authorities."

"I'm not!" Chet shouted. "Fellows, do something!" he begged.

"We'll try," Frank offered. "You and Tony stay here. Come on, Joe. We'll go over to police head-quarters and find out what's wrong."

Chet slumped into a seat. He was dazed by the strange turn of events. "You don't think it's Torres's way of getting even, do you?" he asked Tony.

"Search me," his friend answered, "but it might well be."

Ten minutes passed, and Chet was now pacing up and down the airline office, sighing and muttering to himself. Finally the Hardys returned.

"Make that *four* reservations!" Joe called out cheerfully to the clerk. "Chet, everything's okay. You've been cleared!"

"You mean it? Honest? No foolin'?" Chet could hardly believe his good luck.

"That's right, unless you're a jailbird out on parole."

"What! You know I—"

Frank waved his hand for silence and explained that another Chester Morton, who had just moved to Bayport and was living on a farm at the northern end of the city limits, was out from the state prison on parole!

"You had better get yourself a city address," Joe said. "Otherwise, you might be getting invitations from the prison to drop in once in a while."

Chet, with a wide grin on his pleasant, pudgy face, stepped up and got his ticket and tourist card along with the other boys. They were now advised that their flight was at ten o'clock the following morning. It would land them at one New York airport from which they would go to another field for the journey to Guatemala.

"We'll have to work fast," Frank said, as the boys started for the car. "We'll need both light and heavy clothes."

As the Hardys each packed a suitcase and a duffle bag, their father recommended that they again test their memories on the markings on the two Texichapi medallions. Both had them letter-perfect.

"I think Tony and Chet should also learn them," Frank said, and phoned the boys to come over.

Neither of their friends, however, could seem to memorize the strange markings on the medallions.

"Let me give you a tip," Mr Hardy said. "You begin, Chet. Take a good look at our drawings and then, with your eyes closed, sketch them in your mind. Mark Twain did this to memorize the Mississippi River when he was a young river pilot."

The memory trick worked and soon both boys had memorized the strange lines which the Hardys believed were directions to the treasure.

At eight o'clock Mr Hardy was ready to go out of town on his case. He wished the boys luck on their exciting trip, reminding them to get in touch with Mr Putman's friend at the consulate if they needed help.

"Sam Radley will drive you to the airport and keep his eyes open for suspicious persons interested in your trip."

When Sam Radley appeared the next morning to drive the boys to the airport, he reported that Luis Valez had still admitted nothing and was being held for the federal authorities.

"He may break yet," Frank prophesied.

As he and Joe kissed Mrs Hardy and Aunt Gertrude good-bye, both women came close to shedding tears. "Please take good care of yourselves," their mother pleaded, and their aunt said, "Watch out in those mountains, you could catch your death of cold!"

Sam Radley, in high spirits, cheered up the women with his jokes, then he and the brothers drove off to pick up Tony and Chet. At the airfield Sam showed the boys his new magnifying spectacles.

"Here," he said to Tony with a wink, "put them on

and you'll see a little strand of a girl's hair on Chet's jacket."

The stout boy blushed. "That's not a girl's hair. That's only Iola's." The others roared with laughter.

"I guess you don't miss much with these spectacles," said Tony, after putting them on for a moment. "Sam, you haven't shaved since last night."

The detective laughed. "You're right, of course."

While the boys were waiting for their bags to be weighed, a familiar voice said, "Hello, boys!"

Willie Wortman! The big redhead seemed as jovial as ever. "I missed you by a couple of minutes at your house," he said. "I was up this way and dropped by to see how you were making out about those medallions. I'd sure like to get 'em."

The four boys looked inquiringly at one another. Did he or did he not know anything about what had happened? Tony at once decided to let the Hardys do all the talking. Chet was introduced but said nothing more than "Hi!"

Feeling that secrecy was the best policy, Frank said, "About the medallions, Willie—we've had bad luck."

"That's a shame," Wortman said. "Don't forget about the curse that's on 'em. I expect bad luck to overtake me any time."

The Hardys felt sure that Willie's trip to Bayport had something to do with the man who was now in jail. Watching the seaman closely, Frank said, "Your friend Luis Valez was arrested last night."

"Valez arrested!" Wortman cried out. "What for?" Then the sailor suddenly realized what he had said. His eyes opening wide, he asked, "How did you find out I know Valez? Did he tell you?"

"No." Joe grinned. "We just guessed it."

Wortman took no offence at this. "You *are* good detectives," he said.

Joe went on, "Valez is the fellow who told you about the medallions' curse, isn't he?"

Paling slightly, Wortman nodded. Joe now questioned him about the man with him on the New York street. The seaman denied having been with anyone.

Frank looked straight at Wortman. "Do you know a friend of Valez's who sells kitchen gadgets?"

"No."

Just then the loud-speaker announced that it was time for passengers to board the New York flight.

"Come on," Tony urged.

Frank hung back a moment. "Willie," he said, "that salesman was responsible for us boys and some girls nearly being seriously injured. That's one of the reasons Luis Valez is now in jail. You'd better watch your step about the company you keep!"

The boys moved off, leaving Wortman with his jaw sagging and his eyes popping.

When they reached the gate, Sam Radley was waiting for them. In a loud voice he called, "Have a swell trip, fellows!"

The detective took hold of Frank's arm and pulled him aside. In a quick whisper he said, "Frank. I think there's a Ladino man on the plane masquerading as a woman. I've got a hunch that it has to do with your case. Watch out!"

·19· *The Masquerader*

AMAZED by Sam Radley's warning words about the masquerader on the plane, Frank hurried after the other boys.

"What did Radley tell you?" asked Joe, as the quartet started up the aircraft steps to the cabin. "You look upset."

"Let you know later," Frank whispered.

As the craft flew out over the bay, Frank, pretending to be trying for a better view of the harbour, leaned close to his brother. "Sam Radley thinks there's a Ladino man dressed as a woman on the plane," he whispered tensely. "I guess Sam got a good look at her through his magnifying spectacles and figures she has a shaven face and wears a wig. He thinks this 'woman' may be mixed up in our case."

"Oh, help!" Joe exclaimed under his breath. "But say, what gave Sam the clue to this Ladino stuff?"

"Don't know. That's what I mean to find out."

Sitting back in his seat, Frank joked with Tony. He got up, leaned over his friend's shoulder, and in between laughs told him the news.

"Pass it on to Chet," he whispered. Then Frank started to look through a magazine.

After a moment, Frank arose, saying he was going to talk to the stewardess and incidentally try to spot the suspected person. The three boys watched eagerly as Frank started up the narrow passageway to where the

116

blonde flight hostess was preparing coffee for the passengers.

Halfway there he spotted someone he was sure was the Ladino. The woman was seated alone. Frank wondered if she had purchased both chairs on purpose to keep a seatmate from becoming suspicious. The boy was tempted to sit down alongside her but decided not to.

The suspect had very dark skin and black eyes. She wore a dark-blue dress with a small white collar. Her hair was black with a Spanish-type comb in it. A narrow shawl was pulled round her shoulders. She was reading a book.

"That's a man wearing a wig, all right," Frank thought as he reached the stewardess and asked to see the passenger list.

The Spanish-looking woman was listed as Mrs John Macky, New York City. The adjoining seat was for Mr Macky. A fake reservation, just as Frank had thought!

As Frank was returning to his seat he saw that the so-called Mrs Macky was turning the pages of her book. With a sense of shock, but one that made him almost certain that she was disguised, he noticed that her hands were large and masculine in appearance.

A moment later he said to Joe, "Radley was right. And I have a hunch the fellow in disguise may be Torres minus his moustache. He has a prominent chin, as Dad said."

Joe was thunderstruck. "Do you think Willie was here to see him off?"

"Who knows?" Frank replied. "Anyway, Radley will keep an eye on Willie."

The problem of what strategy to pursue raced

through the Hardys' minds. Was this woman following the boys, or was the masquerade for some completely different reason? Was the suspect really Torres, and did he know that the boys were headed for Texichapi? If so, they should try to elude him and in turn follow him.

At Frank's suggestion he and Tony exchanged places and the Hardys' friends were told of the plans. But Tony did not want to wait to unmask the imposter. "I'm going back there and pull off her wig!" he declared.

"Suppose we're wrong," Joe countered. "We'd better do what Frank suggests."

"What's that?"

"Wait till we arrive in New York before we take any action. Then we'll use an FBI tactic. Let the enemy follow us till he tips his hand. But, in the meantime, we'll give him a false impression of our plans."

When the plane approached the airport, the boys fastened their seat belts, but decided to be the first ones to alight. The wheels touched down gently and the massive craft rolled swiftly towards the passenger terminal.

"Keep together now!" Frank passed the word.

The boys succeeded in being the first to descend the high steps to the runway. Mrs Macky, they took note, was not far behind.

"I'm sure looking forward to a stay at the Kampton Hotel here," Joe said in a loud voice.

Tony carried on the ruse by stating that there were a lot of sights he wanted to see in the city. Actually, the boys planned to climb into a waiting taxicab and be driven to the other airport as originally planned.

Suddenly the boys stopped dead in their tracks.

"Tony Prito!" a loud voice was calling. "Telegram for Tony Prito!"

Seeing the youth hold up his hand, a messenger hurried over, handed him the envelope, and left.

Opening the envelope, Tony pulled out the message. It was not a telegram at all, but a hand-printed warning: *Stay out of Guatemala or your life will be in danger!*

"And the thing's full of ashes!" Chet whispered nervously.

"This settles it," said Frank grimly. "We get out of here as fast as we can."

By this time their luggage had come through and the boys quickly claimed it. Frank whispered directions and they followed him to a coach that would take passengers into the heart of the city. In the line of those waiting stood Mrs Macky!

"We're in luck!" Joe thought elatedly.

The Bayport group waited until the suspect was seated in the coach and other people piling in. Then they made a dash for a waiting taxi and rode off.

Frank directed the driver to the other airport and the taxi was soon speeding towards the plane that was to carry them to Guatemala. As they reached the mammoth, busy airport, Tony began looking round frantically.

"What's up?" Joe asked.

"The number of bags," Tony replied. "We had nine. And now I can count only eight!"

Tony was right. One bag was missing!

"And it's mine!" Tony moaned. "It had all my clothes in it."

"Couldn't we return to the other field?" Chet asked, but Frank pointed out that they could never get back in time to catch the Central American flight.

Tony was grim. "What'll I do?" he asked woefully.

"You'll just have to dress like an Injun!" Joe laughed and folded his arms across his chest Indian style. "You heap big chief of our tribe."

·20· *Volcano!*

THE remark about Tony having to wear Indian garb gave Frank an idea. "That might be a smart thing to do," he said. "In Indian dress, with his black hair and dark skin, Tony might pass for a native guide."

"Sure," Tony agreed. "I might be able to learn things the rest of you couldn't that would help us in our search. Only trouble is," he sighed, "I can't speak any Spanish or Indian dialect."

Frank grinned and Joe said, "Oh, you can act like an anti-social Indian and say nothing."

The boys boarded the plane. Presently the hostess came round with magazines and Tony asked whether she had any literature on Guatemala. The pleasant young woman brought him a book, in which he was soon absorbed.

As the plane took off and the other boys stared out the windows at the ground below, Tony discovered an item of interest in the Guatemalan book. It concerned an eccentric type of Indian, who rarely spoke and roamed the countryside looking for the sacred quetzal bird. "This would make a perfect disguise for me," thought Tony. In another chapter, he studied and memorized some simple, useful words common to all Indians.

Then, excited by the prospect of playing the role of Indian, he showed the book to his friends. After they, too, had read of the bird-searching Indians, Tony flipped back to a page where a picture of the quetzal bird was shown. About the size of a turtle dove, it was emerald green in colour, with a shining crown containing ruby-red and blue tints.

"To keep from disarranging its beautiful, yard-long tail," the caption underneath the picture explained, "the bird builds both an entrance and an exit to its nest."

"Sure is pretty," observed Joe, reading on. "Say, fellows!" he exclaimed. "Listen to this! The bird cannot live in captivity, and is loved by the people for its free, wild, independent spirit. Because of this, the rare quetzal bird has become the national symbol of Guatemala. In ancient times only the chiefs were allowed to wear this bird's exquisite plumage."

Chet sighed. "I'll take a good domestic broiled chicken any day," he remarked, as the others laughed.

The transport plane winged its way down the coast and the four boys finally dozed in their deep, comfortable seats.

At sunrise the plane was over the Caribbean, nearing the eastern coast of Guatemala.

"There's the shore line!" Joe cried, as he noticed that the vivid blue sea water was changing to a lighter hue. A glimpse at the white strip of beach and the mountains beyond excited all the boys.

"I can hardly wait to land!" Frank exclaimed.

At the Guatemala City airfield, the boys were cleared through customs. Then, gathering their bags, they went outside to look for a taxi. A driver approached and introduced himself as Jorge Almeida.

Smiling broadly as he picked up two bags, Almeida said, "This way, *amigos*. I have a fine taxi waiting for you!"

Grinning, they followed his slender but wiry figure to an old open car parked by the kerb. The driver strapped the bags on the running board and the boys got inside.

The affable driver turned round from his seat in the front and said, "Now where shall my little taxi take you?"

"Texichapi," Joe replied with a grin.

Then Chet said, "Better take us to a hotel first—some place where they have good food," he added hopefully.

"Hokay!" Jorge Almeida replied, and like a stock-car racer coming out of the pits, the taxi joined the highway and started speeding towards the city.

As he drove, the man chatted like an over-talkative parrot. He told the boys he knew of no place near Guatemala City named Texichapi. "But," he admitted modestly, "it is possible for it to be somewhere else. I have not been everywhere."

They reached a crossroad and another taxi approached from the highway to the right. Instead of slowing down, Jorge started blowing his horn wildly. Then he stepped on the accelerator and whizzed across the path of the other cab, missing it by inches.

"Brakes no good," Jorge explained, flashing an engaging grin at his dumbfounded passengers. "Don't use much, anyway. Horn much better!"

The boys crossed their fingers for luck, hoping that they would reach the hotel without a car crash. Meanwhile, Jorge pointed out the sights of the plaza, at times leaning far out the side of the cab to indicate a certain place.

"Say, this is better than a Hollywood movie setting," Joe said, chuckling, as Jorge finally slowed down and drove them round the big square and past the arcades where natives sold food from small booths.

In the centre of the plaza, men were arranging chairs on a bandstand in preparation for the evening's concert, Jorge informed his passengers. Gaily dressed pedestrians were strolling along the promenades, admiring the beds of gorgeous, brightly coloured flowers.

"Look at those men!" Joe exclaimed.

A group of small-statured Indians in red serapes, shawl-like blankets thrown over their shoulders, sat crouched in the shade of the arcades. "Tony, that's what you'll look like in your new clothes!"

Tony grunted. "*Sí*, me searchum quetzal bird!"

The others grinned at his odd combination of Spanish and American-Indian dialect.

"Everybody like that bird." Jorge laughed as he circled the square twice and finally stopped at the entrance of a clean, whitewashed hotel near the end of the plaza. "This place hokay!" he announced, unloading the baggage as they got out of the vehicle.

Frank added a generous tip to the taxi fare and Jorge said, "You fine boys! More fun to drive than fat lady tourists!" He laughed. "I drive you cheap from now on—maybe almost free!"

The boys thanked Jorge for this offer, and obtaining his address, promised to get in touch with him when they were ready for another ride.

After checking into the hotel and stowing their gear in two airy bedrooms, the boys set out to learn what they could about the road to Texichapi.

"Look!" Chet exclaimed, pointing out a booth near the square where native dishes were displayed.

"I'm going to get a few *tortillas* and all the fixin's."

The boys then continued walking round the promenade. At the side opposite the hotel, Joe spotted a shop that sold Indian goods. "Let's go in and find a travelling outfit for Tony," he suggested.

While Tony was buying wool trousers and a warm jacket, the other boys had a great deal of fun. Each tried on serapes, moccasins, and embroidered shirts. Finally Tony's costume, including a shoulder-length wig, was wrapped and the group returned to the hotel.

Half an hour later, the quartet appeared on the plaza. Tony made an odd-looking companion in his Indian clothes and wig.

"Now I'm ready for the quetzal bird!" he said, laughing.

A Spanish-looking Ladino, standing nearby, stared darkly at Tony and spat on the ground. Then he savagely spoke a Spanish phrase that Frank understood to mean:

"*A curse on you!*"

As the boys hurried away, Chet said fearfully, "Hadn't we better give up this scheme? You might get all of us in trouble, Tony, pretending to be hunting for their sacred bird."

"I won't mention it again," Tony promised.

After eating lunch in a nearby restaurant Jorge had recommended, the boys hunted up Mr Putnam's friend. To their disappointment, he had gone to Brazil.

"We'll just have to inquire where Texichapi is," said Frank.

But when they did, the various men shook their heads. No one had ever heard of it. A few knew where the Kulkuls lived—in a northwesterly direction from the city, but were vague as to any details about them.

"I guess that we'll have to map out a route to the Kulkul area and take a chance that the Indians will tell us where Texichapi is," Frank concluded.

He bought a road map and the boys pored over it until late that night. A route was finally decided upon.

"We can go one hundred miles to this point in a car," Joe pointed out. "After that, we'll have to try to hire mules to use from there on."

"We'd better let Dad know how we're making out," suggested Frank, and sent an airmail letter to Mr Hardy bringing him up to date on their plans.

The next morning, the hotel clerk was very accommodating and directed them to a food supply store. Here they purchased a quantity of canned goods and bread. In the course of their conversation with the shopkeeper, he remarked that he had a relative at the one-hundred-mile point who rented out mules, saddles, and blankets to tourists who wanted to explore the mountainous country.

"Shall we take a chance on Jorge and his daredevil driving to get us there?" Tony asked, grinning.

"I'm game," Joe replied, "as long as he fixes those brakes."

They got in touch with the native driver. His face became one expansive smile when he was given the assignment. As the boys walked back to the hotel, Joe remarked, "Doesn't it seem queer to you that we haven't been followed or bothered even once by our enemies?"

"How about the one who cursed Tony?" Chet asked.

"I don't think he was part of any gang," Joe replied. "He probably was one of those people who are superstitious about the quetzal bird and thought Tony was making fun of it."

"Don't forget," said Frank, "that we don't know who all our enemies are. We may meet more of them yet. I suggest that we leave here early tomorrow morning before anyone's up."

By phone they completed arrangements with Jorge Almeida and soon after sunrise he was at the hotel entrance. The clothing the boys were not taking was checked at the hotel, and they set off in rough, warm mountain apparel. Tony, in his Indian costume, stowed the two duffle bags inside the taxi.

"You turn Indian?" Jorge grinned. "Almost fool me," he added.

"Good," said Tony. "But I don't know how to manage this blanket!" He grabbed his serape as it started to slip off his shoulders. Jorge explained how Tony could secure it. Then the boys climbed into the car and started their exciting journey to look for the Texichapi treasure.

In high spirits, Jorge sang a witty native tune as the road started to climb into the mountainous country. "Now we make with the speed!" he announced, driving like a daredevil round a sharp turn.

The boys' hair was standing on end as the car screeched round another narrow bend, where the valley dropped away a thousand feet below. "Good-bye, Bayport!" cried Chet, shuddering.

"What the matter?" Jorge asked, between puffs of an aromatic cigarette he was smoking furiously.

"Please take it easy!" Chet moaned.

Just then a great roaring sound rumbled through the mountains. "What's that?" Tony cried.

"Volcano, I think," Jorge replied, concern on his face. "We see."

As the car completed the next sharp turn, the boys gasped in wonder. The mountain-top above them was exploding in a giant fountain of liquid fire! The boiling 2000-degree lava was already pouring down the slope. In a few minutes it would reach the road!

"We're trapped!" cried Chet.

"No, no, we have ten minutes," said Jorge. "We beat it!"

He raced the car along the road, but had gone only a hundred yards when there was another ominous rumble. Then, almost directly in front of the boys, a second eruption gushed up.

"We're lost!" cried Tony, as the lava spray came within a few feet of the car.

"I manage!" Jorge cried. "Beat other fire river before it run across road."

The driver put the gear in reverse, and steered the taxi back along the treacherous roadway.

"We'll never make it!" Chet groaned. "The volcano will get us!"

Sweat poured out on Jorge's swarthy face as he steered the swaying taxi. Could he get beyond the lava flow before it was too late?

·21· A Kidnapped Companion

JORGE ALMEIDA worked desperately to bring his car past the danger area. It swayed and skidded. Once he scraped against the stony mountain wall. With a ripping noise a bumper sheared off.

But Jorge did not slow down. Pressing the accelerator to the floor board, he backed round the serpent-like turn.

"Faster! Faster!" urged Chet, eyeing the hundred-foot-wide, red-hot lava flow above them.

It was so close the boys could feel the intense heat from it.

In a moment it would reach the road. Unless they could get beyond the liquid fire—!

With another burst of speed the taxi shot round the turn. Too late the boys saw that the road was blocked by several massive rocks that had rolled down the mountainside.

"We'll crack up!" Tony yelled.

Jorge braked the speeding car and succeeded in slowing it. But not enough. The taxi smashed into the boulders, throwing the boys violently forward in their seats.

All were dazed by the shock, but managed to climb out of the car. Jorge, who was partly stunned, was pulled out by Joe and Frank. The trio scrambled over the boulders, following Tony and Chet in their desperate flight to get as far away as possible from the taxi which was directly in the path of the fiery lava oozing down the cliff. Seconds later, the destructive stream gushed over Jorge's wrecked car, carrying the taxi with it to the valley below.

"Whew!" sighed Joe, when they stopped running and looked back at the fiery spectacle. "Boy, that was a close call!"

"Y-yes," stammered Chet, dropping exhausted to the roadway.

"Thank goodness we're all safe!" said Frank.

"All but my little taxi," moaned Jorge. Then suddenly his face brightened. "It's hokay! We got insurance. I will get new taxi from the company," he said, "with louder horn."

"But what'll *we* do?" asked Chet. "We've lost our supplies and equipment. All that food," he moaned.

"We get more!" Jorge said cheerfully.

Both Frank and Joe looked doubtful, for they did not share his lightheartedness. They were miles from any city or town and now had no means of transportation.

"My cousin, Alvero Montero, owns *fianca*," he said. "It is long distance back but we can walk it easily. He has mules we can borrow."

The boys gladly accepted the offer and followed Jorge down the mountainside. For the remainder of the day, they trekked through the thick undergrowth of the valley. Chet was the first to start complaining of hunger.

"It's six hours since our last meal," he moaned, "and all that food buried in the lava. If I don't find something soon, I'll have to turn cannibal and eat one of you."

"Huh," said Joe, "your teeth aren't that good. Haven't you found out how tough we are?"

Shortly before dusk, the group arrived at the charming, typically Spanish Montero plantation. Work had ended for the day, and as the boys approached, the aroma of cooking meat, onion and spices reached them.

A tall, pleasant-looking man, dressed in work clothes, appeared at the front of the main house.

"My cousin," said Jorge, and hooted a signal to his relative.

Montero waved and hurried to meet his unexpected

guests. "Welcome, Jorge!" he cried in Spanish. "You bring friends? Good. You are all just in time to take dinner with us."

Then, as the group came closer, he noticed their dishevelled condition. "You have been in a battle with rebels?" he continued. "And what are you doing on foot? Where is your taxi, Jorge?"

Almeida introduced the boys and told his cousin of the near tragedy. After expressing his sympathy, the planter looked in amusement at Tony's disguise. "You had me fooled." Montero laughed. "And I see Indians every day. They work here."

The planter invited the group inside and presented the boys to his beautiful Spanish wife and their two small sons. He provided the visitors with swimming trunks, and the men and boys swam in the cold, clear mountain water of a dammed-up stream near the house. Later, they sat down to eat a lavish steak dinner.

Chet could hardly listen to the conversation as he eyed the platters of juicy meat. The hungry boys had never tasted a better meal, especially the dessert— bowls piled high with papayas and pineapples.

After the meal, Mr Montero, smoking a slender black cigar, told the boys that he had never heard of Texichapi. But he would be glad to lend them four mules to take them to the point where they planned to rent animals and equipment for the rest of their trip.

"If anyone in Guatemala knows about Texichapi," Montero continued, "it will be a remarkable old Indian who lives in a village across the next mountain. You'll go through it."

"Will he talk to us?" Frank asked.

"Yes," Montero replied. "His name is Tecum-Uman. Tell him I sent you—he knows me well."

Jorge arranged with his cousin to let the travellers stay overnight and they all slept soundly. Early in the morning he excused himself, saying he would go back to Guatemala City on one of Alvero's mules and report the loss of his car to the taxi company. A few minutes later he was riding away on a cocoa-brown burro, waving in his cheerful, carefree way.

"Good luck, *amigos*!" he called, just before he disappeared round a turn.

The Hardys and their friends prepared to start for the village where Tecum-Uman lived. Mr Montero gave them a supply of food and handed each boy a machete. "With this, you can chop your way through the thickets."

Thanking the planter for all the favours he had shown them and saying good-bye to his family, the boys mounted their animals. Mr Montero said that the mules could be left at the place where the boys would pick up the others. Two of his plantation workers would bring them back later.

With Tony still wearing the Indian outfit, the quartet began their arduous ride. Because the road was cut off, they were forced to take a path through the dense forest of the valley.

"I wish we had a guide with us," Chet remarked.

"What do we need a guide for," Joe asked, "when we have Big Chief Tony? He will lead us to Tecum-Uman."

"*Sí*, we no get lost, *amigos*," Tony said with a stony face. "Only trouble is, wig itches!" He scratched his head and laughed.

The talk shifted to the treasure.

"What do you think it is?" Chet asked.

Frank said, "I've read that when Cortez's captain,

Alvarado, conquered this country over four hundred years ago, he reported that the Indians had great quantities of gold and precious jewels. Some of this treasure was buried by earthquakes, floods, and volcanic eruptions, and people have been searching for it ever since."

"Don't let your hopes soar too high," said Joe. "You may end up with some worthless three-eyed stone monsters."

Several times along the way, the quartet overtook small groups of homeless refugees whose houses and land had been devastated by the same volcano which nearly cost the boys their lives.

Each time the boys met these groups, Tony tried out his dialect, asking the people about the location of Texichapi. To his delight, they understood him and seemed to accept him as a member of some other tribe, but the boys were disappointed not to learn anything about Texichapi from the natives.

Travelling at a brisker pace than the heavily laden people, the boys quickly moved out ahead of the refugees. In mid-afternoon, as they approached the Indian village where they thought Tecum-Uman might live, the four riders came upon another group of natives on the narrow trail. Tony prepared to try out his disguise once again.

As the group rode up, the mounted Indians suddenly spotted Tony and cried out frantically, *"Shaman! Shaman!"*

They made a quick, flanking movement and encircled the stunned boys. Before Tony could even open his mouth, the attackers had grabbed him, pulled him on to a horse ridden by the fiercest-looking of the lot, and galloped off.

"They've kidnapped him!" Chet cried out.

• 22 • *The Weird Ceremony*

As Chet made a mad dash after Tony's kidnappers, Frank called him back.

"What's the big idea?" the boy cried, returning to the brothers. To his amazement, they wore broad grins.

"How can you stand there laughing when Tony's in trouble? Why don't we *do* something instead of just looking?"

"Calm down, Chet," Joe said. "Didn't you hear what those Indians were yelling when they captured Tony?"

"It sounded like *shaman*," Chet replied.

"Exactly," Frank said. "And that means sooth-sayer." Shading his eyes from the sun the Hardy boy peered ahead. "Looks as if they're taking Tony to the village. They probably think he's some sort of travelling magic man."

"Oh," Chet sighed in relief.

Joe, however, was worried. "I sure hope Tony can get away with it," he reflected. "If they find out he's not a shaman—"

"Suppose we all wander into the village," Frank proposed. "By the time we get there they'll probably have elected Tony chief of the tribe!"

With Joe leading Tony's mule, the little procession started along the trail.

"What's so wonderful about a shaman?" Chet questioned.

"He's a mixture of priest and poet," Frank replied. "Whatever the shaman says goes. He is supposed to be able to see into the future. One ritual he performs is called 'telling the mixes.' "

"What's that?" Chet asked eagerly.

"When a person plans to do something on a certain day," Frank explained, "and he wants to be sure it's the right time, he calls on a shaman. This man arranges some red beans from a pita tree—"

"Did you say Prito?" Chet interrupted.

"No." Frank laughed. "I said pita. Then he burns some stuff called copal, says his mumbo-jumbo and announces to the man whether it's the lucky day or not."

"We could use a shaman for our Bayport football schedule," Joe remarked with a laugh.

Suddenly the trail turned sharply into the cobbled main street of the village. Adobe shacks with thatched roofs lined both sides. Just as in Guatemala City, the Indians here, too, huddled against the poles that supported the shop roofs.

"You know, in those red bandannas and felt hats," Joe remarked, "those fellows look just like Tony in disguise."

There was no sign of their friend or of the group that had borne him off. But Frank felt certain that the Indians would release Tony as soon as they discovered their mistake.

"While we're waiting, let's ask one of these men about Tecum-Uman," he suggested.

Frank went along the line asking the same question of each of the stolid, poker-faced natives. He got only a cold stare in return.

"Well, that idea went over like a lead balloon," he said a bit angrily. "Let's look for Tony."

At the end of the street stood a low, whitewashed building with a long porch. It looked like a shop. Half a dozen natives were moving about in front of the place, which appeared to be the only spot in the village with any activity.

"That must be where they took Tony," Joe said.

"Unless they have some kind of a temple," Frank added.

"Let's try this place, anyway," Chet urged.

The trio rode to the end of the street and dismounted near the building. At first the natives paid little attention to the boys. But when Joe walked up to a man near the door and asked him in Spanish if he might go in and look round, the native scowled. He shook his head as if he did not understand Spanish and made a threatening gesture.

"Don't get tough," Joe said in English. "I'll just walk in."

"Careful, Joe!" Frank called.

But his brother reached for the knob. At once two Indians stepped up, one on each side of the boy and struck him across the cheeks with the butt of their hard, bony hands. The force of the unexpected blows caused Joe to lose his balance and fall backwards. Furious, he picked himself up and rushed at the bigger Indian, punching him soundly on the jaw.

"That was a beauty!" Frank cried.

The man's eyes glazed and his knees sagged, then he dropped with a half-turn to the porch.

"We'll take this one!" Frank yelled as he swept past Joe to meet the charge of the second Indian. Dodging a vicious blow, Frank swiftly crouched, grabbed the man round the knees, and hurled him to the floor. As Frank leaped to his feet and turned to his brother, the doors of the building were flung wide open. Through the entrance swarmed the whole group of kidnappers. Seeing their guards lying stunned on the floor, the angered Indians attacked the boys. The three friends fought violently but, being greatly outnumbered, were overwhelmed and quickly bound.

The kidnappers, who had not spoken a word, led them through the doorway. Here other natives were carrying armfuls of mahogany wood to the centre of the large main room. Other men sat silently in a circle. This was not a shop after all, but some kind of ceremonial hall. Tony was not in sight. The captured boys were taken to the centre of the circle.

"Look, they're starting a fire!" Chet's face turned white when he saw an old man step forward from the circle and ignite the chips. The stout boy gulped. "They're going to use us as human sacrifices!" he cried, panic-stricken.

Standing inside the ring of about forty Indians who sat glowering at them, the Hardys whispered words of encouragement to each other and to Chet.

"But look!" he gasped. "They're coming after us! They'll toss us into the fire!"

The men walked past the boys, however, and went for more wood which they laid across the blaze.

Some of the smoke was escaping through an opening in the roof, but the place was already hazy. The three boys began to cough.

"Maybe this is part of the curse that Willie Wortman warned us about!" Chet moaned. "We'll never get out of here alive!"

Frank, trying to keep up his courage, said he was

afraid that the Indians had overheard the boys talking about the treasure. If this were the case and he could convince them that they did not intend to steal any of it, the boys might go free. But before Frank had a chance to try to find out, Joe suddenly exclaimed, "I think Chet was right! Look what's happening now!"

The men in the circle began to chant on a single low note. Without getting any louder, they continued to chant for many minutes. Then two drummers entered the circle and started in accompaniment to the singing.

"If only someone would say something!" Joe burst out.

The sound of the beating drums grew louder. The men seated in the ring made rhythmic motions with their hands. The chanting increased in fervour—louder and louder, until the boys could no longer hear each other speak.

The singing became an angry, wild outcry that sounded like war-dance music. Snake-like, the circle came to life as the men, one by one, slowly rose to their feet and started stamping, sending clouds of dust swirling off the dirt floor into the smoky blue atmosphere.

At the entrance to the building, there now appeared four weirdly painted dancers wearing feathered headdresses. With a savage throbbing of the drums, these half-naked Indians, brandishing long spears, leaped through space into the moving circle of stamping fanatics. As they whirled past the boys, the prisoners could see the milk-white and scarlet streaks of paint on the dancers' faces and the eerie blue lines daubed along their sweating shoulders.

"*Kai-ee tamooka! Kai-ee tamooka!*" the entire circle bellowed as the big dance got under way.

The solo dancers moved to the right as the circle stamped clockwise. Dust and smoke almost blinded the boys. The drummers started a faster beat that sounded as if it would tear the skin off their instruments. The chanting became a half-scream.

Then, as if by some invisible signal, the wild frenzy came to a sudden end. The performers stood as if frozen. Not a muscle of a single man moved. Then a slow thump—thump—thumping of a lone drum began. Slowly the men in the circle reformed their ring and crouched in silence on the dirt floor. A moment later the circle moved in on the boys and the dying fire.

Now the oldest man rose and approached the low-burning fire. With his arms extended, palms up, he stood for several moments without uttering a sound. Then, as several of the elder members of the circle began to murmur some gibberish, the leader pulled a long stick from a sheath. With it he poked about in the embers. Scraping carefully, he heaped up a cone-shaped pile like those the boys had seen before!

The chanting ceased. The circle closed even smaller. The leader extended his arms a second time and the murmuring began again, a little louder than before. Now, with his stick, the man scraped some of the warm ashes into a wooden bowl.

"*Kai-ee! Kai-ee!*" The chant picked up volume and the leader turned from the fire to face the Hardys and Chet. Holding the bowl out stiffly, chest high, he stopped directly in front of the boys. Inwardly quaking, the captives tried to appear unperturbed.

Murmuring the chant himself, the old Indian sprinkled the hot ashes on the foreheads of the trio. The boys winced as the fragments struck their bare skin but did not cry out.

There was a sudden commotion at the entrance. Then came a booming, commanding voice over the heads of the people, The leader, lowering the bowl, cried out:

"*Tecum-Uman!*"

The man for whom the boys had been searching! What would happen to them now?

·23· *Into Dangerous Country*

A HANDSOME, elderly Indian, taller than the other tribesmen, walked with stately steps towards the Hardys and Chet. He motioned to a native that they be unbound at once.

After this was done, the tall Indian addressed Frank in Spanish. "Do you speak this language?"

"A little," Frank replied, then hastened to ask, "Where is our friend? Is he all right?"

For the first time a faint smile played round the Indian's mouth. "He is quite safe. He is changing his clothes and will be brought here shortly. Your mules, also, are unharmed."

Frank told the other boys this news, then said, "I don't understand what has happened, Tecum-Uman. We were advised to ask your aid by Señor Montero."

"Yes," the elderly man nodded. "The Señor is an old friend of mine. I am sorry you have been poorly treated here."

Mystified, Frank asked him to explain the reasons for the odd happenings they had just experienced. For answer, Tecum-Uman motioned for the boys to follow him outside. Reaching a secluded spot, the man turned again to Frank and began to speak.

"I am chief of the three Kulkul Indian villages," he said. "This village is one of them but not where I live. I came here because certain men have been causing much trouble. They are the ones who captured young Prito and took you into the ceremonial hall."

Tecum-Uman explained that he was sure a certain dishonest Ladino in the area was responsible for the recent unrest in the village. "I believe he was the man who told my tribesmen that your friend was disguised as a shaman. This thing is regarded as a great evil by my people," he concluded. "The fire dance you witnessed is an old custom performed to break such a curse."

Frank said he regretted the misunderstanding. "Our reason for coming here," he told the chief, "is to find Texichapi. Do you know where it is?"

If the Kulkul chief was surprised by the question, he did not show it.

"Texichapi—as it is called by the Kulkuls—is reputed to be a day's walk west of the place where Prito said you were to get fresh mules and supplies." Tecum-Uman gave no further information. "You will be free to go with your friend when he arrives here. My loyal tribesmen wish you no harm."

As the old man concluded his statement, Tony Prito was led towards them. Dressed in a blue cotton shirt and a pair of nondescript but clean brown trousers, he rushed up to the boys.

"Am I glad to see you!" he cried. "I thought all of us were goners."

"S-so did we!" Chet stammered.

There was no sign of the unfriendly natives as

Tecum-Uman accompanied the boys to their mules. As a gesture of good will, he handed the boys a sack of food and repeated the directions to Texichapi.

"You will arrive at the village where you change mules and equipment within one hour," Tecum-Uman said. "If you do not leave this trail, you cannot miss it."

The four travellers expressed hearty thanks for his help, and the elderly man waved good-bye to them. As they rode away, the boys told Tony about their ordeal in the whitewashed building and about Tecum-Uman's explanation of it.

"He sure arrived at that clambake in the nick of time," Joe said. "Now tell us what happened to you."

Tony sobered. "This shaman business was a fake," he said. "They knew right away I wasn't an Indian. What they wanted was to find out why we're here. They sure made it hard for me—tried several torture tricks. I guess I can thank Tecum-Uman that things weren't any worse. He arrived in the midst of it. But the guys that were holding me warned that if I told the chief anything, it would go badly with me later."

The Hardys were afraid that the group might be followed and urged their mules forward at a faster pace to outdistance any enemy native runners. Several times Frank dismounted and put his ear to the ground to detect any sounds of horsemen trailing them, but he heard nothing.

"I guess we're safe," he concluded.

Exactly as the old man had predicted, the boys arrived at the next village in one hour. They sought out the shopkeeper's relative who rented mules. He made arrangements for the group to remain overnight, and promised to have their mounts ready for an early-morning start.

After buying fresh supplies for the trip, the boys were shown to the cabin where they were to sleep. The four agreed that they would ask no questions about Texichapi while they stayed in the village.

"We can't tell friend from foe in these mountains," Frank said, "so we'd better just be mum about the treasure."

Before the sun went down, the boys took a short walk round the trading post, inspecting the various supplies that were bought by traders, explorers, and settling farmers. Chet picked up a short-handled miner's shovel.

"Say, here's a tool we might need in Texichapi!" he exclaimed, unwittingly breaking the pledge to silence concerning their destination that the boys had made.

An Indian standing nearby flashed a strange look at Chet. The boys expected him to vanish in the next instant and bring back reinforcements to harm them. But instead the man walked closer and spoke to them in broken Spanish.

"Texichapi?" he asked. "You going there?"

Since Chet had already given away their destination, the boys admitted that they were.

"Bad place," the Indian told them. "Stay away from Texichapi. It is valley of evil."

The man said that Texichapi was hard on a man physically because of its sudden and extreme changes in temperature.

"And besides," he went on, "there are many mahogany trees in Texichapi which are protected by spirits. When someone not wanted tries to enter that section, a curse is put on him!"

The boys looked at one another, dismayed. But the part about the curse did not seem to ring true.

"Where did you learn about the curse?" Frank asked the Indian. The man failed to understand his stilted high school Spanish.

For the next ten minutes, the Hardys and their friends tried to get the native to tell them whether this tale of the curse and the place being called the valley of evil was an old legend of the Indians or whether it was just a recent man-made story. It might be another stratagem of the boys' enemies, the patriotic society, to frighten away the quartet.

"No, sorry," the Indian replied time after time.

"The more I think about going into the Kulkuls' valley," Chet said waveringly, "or about being left behind here, I go cold all over."

The Indian drifted away and the boys returned to their cabin. All were uneasy about going to sleep, not knowing what might happen. But nothing disturbed them except the howling of wild animals in the nearby forest.

At the crack of dawn, the group headed west as Tecum-Uman had instructed them. There was no indication that they were being followed. The boys pushed on and did not take a break in their difficult journey until the sun was directly overhead. Then they lunched briefly on their new provisions and set off again.

Much of the way seemed to be along dry river beds and across streams which appeared to have changed course and left their former beds to flow in adjacent ravines.

"There sure are a lot of crisscrossing trails," observed Frank, who was leading the cavalcade. "The trail to

Texichapi would be mighty tough to follow if Tecum-Uman had not insisted that we keep heading straight west all the time."

Suddenly he stopped, and as the others waited, dismounted and picked up a stick. With it Frank scratched several marks in the dirt. Finishing the last line, he asked the others to look at what he had drawn. "Do these seem familiar?" he asked.

The boys studied the lines for only a few moments, then Joe exclaimed, "Of course. They're the ones on the medallions!"

Frank explained that he had traced the curves of the several streams that they had just passed. "They exactly match the lines that we memorized! We must be in the middle of the Texichapi country!"

Joe looked around excitedly. "I wonder what the opal really meant—should we look for a certain tree, a cave, or maybe a particular hill?"

No one knew the answer. Taking their bearings on the curve of the last stream, the boys changed course slightly. For half a mile they beat their way through swampy ground until they saw, sparkling like a jewel, a small lake at the base of a distant cliff.

"Do you think this lake corresponds to the location of the opal on the medallion?" asked Tony.

"I doubt that the treasure would be buried underwater," replied Frank. "Besides, we have to travel a little farther if my memory is correct."

The riders broke into a jog as the wooded countryside became more open. Within a few minutes they arrived at the lake.

"Look up there!" Joe cried suddenly.

Two figures stood at the top of a sheer wall of rock that dropped seventy or eight feet straight down to the water. The sight of people in this apparently uninhabited area startled the boys.

As the figures moved close to the rim of the cliff, the watchers could see that they were an Indian man and a small boy.

Frank was about to shout to the Indian when they saw the little boy break away from the man and run along the cliff's edge. They could hear the man give a warning shout. Abruptly, the little boy turned to face the man, but lost his balance and hurtled towards the water.

The four boys gasped in horror as the small form struck the lake surface and disappeared. They realized that, even if the youngster knew how to swim, a fall from such a height would knock the wind out of him and he would drown. The same would be true of the child's companion if he should dive in and attempt a rescue.

"I'm going after that boy!" Joe cried. Slipping off his moccasins and jacket, he dived into the lake!

·24· Followed!

As Joe dived into the lake, his friends watched with concern from the water's edge. Would he be able to reach the drowning child in time? There was still no sign of the boy who had fallen from the cliff.

"Perhaps it's already too late," Joe thought fearfully as he swam underwater with strong, sure strokes.

Suddenly Joe saw the boy. His limp body was entangled in the branches of a sunken tree trunk. Relieved, but with the air in his lungs almost gone, Joe swam over and frantically tried to release the unconscious boy. Just as Joe felt his lungs might burst, the branches gave way, and grasping the child firmly, he quickly rose to the surface.

As Joe emerged into the brilliant sunlight and inhaled great gulps of air, Frank cried out, "Great! Over here, Joe!"

His brother, still clutching the helpless child, headed for shore. As he drew near, Frank jumped into the water and said, "I'll take him!"

He reached for the little boy and carried him ashore. Then he laid the child on the ground and he and Tony began artificial respiration to force the water from his lungs. A few minutes later Chet took a turn.

Presently the Indian who had been on the cliff appeared, tears streaming from his eyes. Jabbering in a language unintelligible to the boys and gesticulating, he indicated that the youngster was his son.

As the water was forced from the little boy's mouth, his limbs began to twitch, and his breathing became more regular. Soon the child's eyes opened. Through gestures, Frank indicated to the Indian that his son was definitely out of danger, but should be put to bed for the rest of the day.

When the child was ready to travel, his father gently picked him up. The man, his face beaming with gratitude, nodded to each boy, then started homeward.

"That was a great rescue you made, Joe," Chet praised his pal, "You've made a real friend of that Indian."

Joe blushed and started removing his wet clothes. The warm breeze quickly dried them. After putting them back on, he said, "All set? Let's head for the treasure spot of Texichapi."

The four riders started towards the place, which, according to the stranger at the trading centre, had the power to cast an evil spell. After making two wrong turns, they finally rode into an area which matched the one on the medallions.

"Why, it's beautiful here!" Tony exclaimed.

"Not windy and cold like that Indian said. And it certainly is cheerful," Chet added, watching the brilliantly coloured birds which flitted among the trees.

Small clumps of spruce filled the valley, and as the mules moved silently over the pine-needled ground, the boys breathed in the crisp air.

"There's a big stand of mahogany trees ahead!" Frank said excitedly. "And that's the spot indicated on the map by the opal."

Eagerly the boys urged their mounts towards it. Reaching the grove of giant trees, they held a conference about where to begin their digging. Frank took a pad from his pocket and once more sketched all the lines from the medallions. Then he sketched in the exact location of the opal.

"At the centre of this gem is where we start digging," he announced and marked the exact area. Then he tore the paper into small bits and scattered them in the breeze.

During the next five hours the boys dug without interruption. Nothing came to light. Finally, tired from the heavy work, they were about to quit for the day when Tony's pick struck a hard surface. It made a slightly different sound from that of the rocks he had come against before.

"Fellows," he said excitedly, "start shovelling here!" Working furiously the group gradually made out the shape of first one, then another heavy stone step leading into the earth.

"This is the beginning!" Joe cried. "Let's really dig!"

Into the dusk, then after a brief night's rest, all through the next morning, the quartet continued their excavation work. After uncovering a dozen steps with a carved balustrade, they came to a stone of a different type.

"I don't think this is a step," said Frank. "It's a slab laid across something."

They decided to prise the slab loose. This proved to be a backbreaking job, but at last they managed to up-end the slab. Below it were more steps, almost free of earth.

Their hearts pounding, the boys beamed their lights ahead and descended. "I feel as if I were walking back through the centuries," Frank commented in a whisper.

In a few moments he and his companions found themselves standing in the anteroom of a huge building. "This must have been a palace!" Joe cried excitedly, as his light picked up carved columns, benches, and walls.

As they made their way through richly carved reception rooms, altar rooms, and finally reached the vast throne room, Chet broke the stillness to exclaim, "Wowee! What a treasure!" The frescoed walls and throne were of solid gold!

"Look at those chairs!" Tony gasped.

The carved seats were inlaid with varicoloured woods. Opals and costly jade crowned the backs of each. Emeralds and rubies glistened from their settings in the golden throne. Eight-foot vases with mosaic figures of Aztec royalty filled the corners of the room.

"These treasures are certainly government property!" Frank said. "No one must be allowed to steal them. We must notify the Guatemalan government at once."

Retracing their steps towards the exit, the boys saw one entire room filled with golden figures. Some were of Aztec men, others of animals and birds.

"Why, this one room alone is worth a fortune!" Joe exclaimed. "No wonder Torres and Valez were ready to kill us to obtain the medallions. If they get hold of this treasure, they'll be the richest men on this side of the world!"

Passing through the reception room hung with tapestries of golden thread woven through the brilliant plumage of tropical birds, the boys approached the steps.

"It seems darker here than when we came down," Tony remarked.

It was true, and the reason soon became obvious to the boys. Several shadowy forms were standing guard at the entrance! Some of them were the boys' tormentors from the Kulkul village, others were white men.

"They've followed us here," Frank whispered. "Even the masquerading 'woman' from the plane!" he groaned. "I recognize his face."

These words were no sooner spoken than the man stepped forward. He announced himself as Alberto Torres, leader of the "patriots". Torres was now dressed in a red-and-white wool shirt and khaki trousers. Smirking, he said:

"I am glad to see the detectives from the States. Of

course it will be impossible for you to escape," he added in a sneering tone. "Permit me to thank you for leading us to the treasure we have sought for so long."

Torres went on, "And now that the fabled treasure has been located, we have no time to lose. You boys will be sealed inside this palace to die while we go for more equipment."

As if the power he held over the boys suddenly inflated him, Torres began to strut before them, talking fast as he walked. "I fooled you all, you and your father," he boasted. "That Valez—he is as stupid as you to let himself be caught. Maybe all detectives in the States are dumb. And that Willie Wortman is dumb too. He sells the medallions—the key to this treasure."

"Where did the medallions come from?" Frank spoke up.

"I can at least amuse you before you die by answering some of your stupid questions," the pompous leader replied. "To begin with, those medallions were cleverly and secretly made by an old Kulkul Indian who had wandered away from his tribe. Most likely he had discovered the treasure and made the medallions as a future guide for Tecum-Uman. He died suddenly in the forest and Wortman's buddy found them on the body of the old Indian. He showed them to me. When I realized later that they must be of great value, I tried to get them from Wortman's friend. But he had disappeared with the medallions.

"I sent Luis Valez," he continued, "to find the fellow who had them. He learned that Willie Wortman had received them in the meantime and sold them to Roberto Prito in New York. Valez went there, then on to Bayport. Willie Wortman, meanwhile, had begun to suspect something, and he too began to search for the medallions."

"Were you the man who got away from me in New York?" Joe interrupted.

"I was," Torres replied in a grand manner. "When Valez seemed to be failing in his mission," he continued, "I hunted up Willie Wortman in New York. I was following him that day when you saw us. I didn't find out anything from him, so I went to Bayport to check on Valez. He was in jail and I learned you were coming to Guatemala, so I took the same plane to New York. You got away at the airport, but I took the next plane down here."

Torres's statement that he had arrived in Bayport after his henchman's arrest cleared up one of the questions in the minds of the Hardys. He was not the man who had helped Valez when he had waylaid Joe and stolen the opal medallion.

"How did you find out we were coming to Guatemala?" Frank asked.

"I learned about it from a friend of mine at the consulate in New York. The patriotic society kept track of you. They traced you through a Guatemala City taxicab company and found that you were already headed out here to the hills."

"Did you arrange what happened to us at the fire ceremony?" Frank queried.

"Yes. And one of my spies tried to keep you from this place by telling you that it is a valley of evil."

After a pause, Torres added, "Tecum-Uman himself hates me, but I have many friends in one of his villages. I sent word to them to bring you in and torture you. The old man of course knew nothing of this. But when he showed up he was told a story of his people having to break a curse you had brought them because of a false shaman."

"You didn't plan on our leaving that village," Joe said.

"No. I was going to get the truth out of you about the treasure right there. But it does not matter. You found it for us, anyway."

"It's too bad," Frank said, "that Tecum-Uman doesn't have a loyal following in all his villages. He'd drive a thief like you right out of the country."

"I warn you," Torres responded angrily, "no more talk like that or I won't even bother to seal you in! I'll kill you right now!" He started pacing again.

Frank, stalling for time and hoping that the boys could think of some way to outwit Torres and escape, questioned the vain man again. "How about the first medallion that Valez stole?" he asked.

The leader of the so-called patriotic society stopped pacing, whirled round, and asked Frank to repeat the question. Frank did as Torres commanded.

"You say he stole it!"

"Yes."

"That dirty double-crosser!" Torres roared. "He was playing his own game and must still have the medallion. Valez never told me he got it. The skunk!"

In spite of Frank's attempt to stall for time, Torres, ruffled by the news of Valez's betrayal, suddenly yelled, "Enough of this delay! Strip these four of their tools and seal them in!"

The leader headed for the steps, and without looking back, climbed the steps to ground level. The six guards closed in!

The Secret Revealed

"OUR only chance is to slug it out with them," whispered Frank. The other boys grimly agreed, though Tony pointed out that they were weaponless and outnumbered.

Quickly the boys retreated to the middle of the room and braced themselves for attack. Two of the enemy headed for Joe, who ducked, grabbed one native's arm, and swiftly slung him jujitsu fashion over his shoulder. The man crashed against a heavy stone idol and lay dazed. Joe's second opponent caught the boy square on the chest and the two fell, rolling over and over.

Chet, knocked to the floor by a husky Indian, decided to use strategy. As the native above him closed in, the boy pretended to let himself be taken. The man relaxed and motioned for Chet to stand up. As he rose, Chet brought the back of his head up flush under the jaw of the unsuspecting enemy, who at once collapsed.

"Two down—four to go!" cried Chet, running towards Tony, who was being backed into a corner. Remembering a recent movie he had seen with Tony, Chet cried out, "Smash!"

At once Tony reached out with both hands and caught the coarse black hair of the man nearest him. Chet did the same to another Indian. With a quick, jerking motion the boys banged the skulls of the natives together with such a crack that the two dropped in a heap, unconscious.

Tony and Chet now looked to see what was happening to the Hardys. Joe was still struggling with his man and Frank was being beaten by the biggest of the attacking group.

"Come on, Chet!" yelled Tony, racing across the room. With only two natives left to subdue, the boys had a chance for escape!

But just then six more Indians swarmed down the steps. There was nothing for the boys to do but surrender. They were lashed tightly together, then laid at the foot of the steps.

The bandits were jubilant! Shouting words of self-praise, they started up the steps. Suddenly, in the bright light of the opening, an Indian with drawn bow appeared on the steps. He let fly with the arrow. One of the bandits screamed in pain as the flint arrowhead seared into his raised right arm.

Several Indians came running down the steps after their leader. Herding the boys' captors into a corner, they ordered one of them to release Frank and Tony from their bonds and then helped Joe and Chet to their feet.

"We're mighty glad to see you!" Frank said. "But where did you come from?"

"Kulkul village," was the reply.

"But how did you know—" Frank began.

Joe interrupted Frank's question by pointing to the steps. The boys turned to look. At the top of the stairs, with broad smiles on their faces, stood the little boy the Hardys had rescued and his father.

"There's our answer!" Joe cried.

The quartet rushed up the steps to thank the man. Again the grateful native tried to explain, using sign language, but failing in this, he asked one of his friends who could speak a little broken English to act as interpreter.

"He say after you save boy he see you go on path to Texichapi. He start to worry," the man began.

"But how did he know we were coming here after the treasure?" Joe asked.

"He not know that. He know we have some bad people in one Kulkul village. When he see them after you, he run to loyal Kulkuls and tell us come quick with him. Our village not far away."

"We want to thank you and all the loyal Kulkuls for saving our lives," Frank said, shaking the spokesman's hand.

"Tomas, the boy's father, he say we even—equal," the man replied. "You save boy. We save you."

A moment later they saw Tecum-Uman approaching the buried palace. He told the boys that Torres and his gang were under guard, awaiting the arrival of the federal police. He added that he had already sent a messenger to inform the officials.

"You boys have done a noble act for the Guatemalan government," the old man said to Frank as he excitedly started on a tour through the palace with the discoverers.

"Yes," the interpreter added, "place belong to ancestor. Thank you for find. Nobody steal. Sacred for government fathers."

The boys led the way through the wealth and beauty of the rooms they had already seen. The Indians were overcome with joy as they saw the splendour of their earlier civilization. Tears of happiness filled Tecum-Uman's eyes.

"With Torres arrested and in jail," the old man said, "the Kulkul tribe will become united again. And this wonderful palace can be restored. The tribal gods have looked on us with favour."

As they moved along, playing their flashlights from one priceless object to another, Chet, who had been leaning against a jewel-panelled wall, suddenly cried, "Hey, what's this?" as the panel swung open. "A whole new passageway!"

Eagerly the boys beamed their lights into this area. On their previous trip through they had thought this decorated rectangle was part of a solid wall.

Tecum-Uman and the others accompanied them into the newly found section. The old man's eyes glistened as he explained to the boys that this must have been a sacred ceremonial room. It was fashioned of pale-pink granite, which probably had been transported from South America, Tecum-Uman explained. Here, too, were costly idols made of beautifully carved woods, silver, or gold set with precious jewels.

The inspection ended, the party retraced their way through the palace and climbed the steps to the sunlight. Across a small clearing the notorious Torres, guarded by several Indians, stood staring glumly at the ground. At the sight of the boys, the leader of the criminals flew into a rage again.

"I will get my revenge!" he yelled. In spite of the Kulkuls' efforts to silence him, he continued screaming at the boys.

"Say, Torres," Chet called, "next time you impersonate a woman, remember to wear gloves—your hands gave you away!"

Torres, incensed by Chet's remark, clenched his large fists and increased his shouting. But a moment later, when reinforcements of loyal Kulkuls ran into the clearing, the man became silent. Tecum-Uman told the boys that they had nothing to worry about concerning further trouble with Torres and his gang.

Posting a guard at the entrance to the palace, the tribal chief asked the boys to get their mules and walk with him at the head of a procession back to the nearby Kulkul village.

"You are heroes," he said, "and my people will want to thank you. But tell me how you learned of this treasure."

The Hardys explained about the medallions and Torres. When they finished the story, Tecum-Uman nodded his head. He said that an elderly member of his tribe had been taken ill while on a hunting trip and died before he could get back to his village. The old man probably was the Indian from whom Willie Wortman's sailor friend had got the medallions.

The exciting news of the Hardy's discovery of the long-buried palace and the arrest of the law-breaker Torres turned the sleepy village into a buzzing bee-hive. Everywhere the usually silent natives talked excitedly about the details that trickled in ahead of the heroes.

"Tecum-Uman, he say big celebration to honour four boys," a panting messenger had told the villagers, running from house to house.

Immediately, all of the Indians' brightly-coloured finery was brought out. Women adorned themselves in gay festival dresses and prepared great dishes of food for the banquet.

Meanwhile, the menfolk had built fires in the bar-becue pits and started roasting chunks of tender beef and pork on the turning spits. The children linked fresh flowers into streamers and strung them above the entrance to the village. Each cottage flew the Guatemalan flag. Musicians tuned up their primitive instruments and waited the arrival of the heroes. By the time the Hardys arrived with Chet and Tony, everything was ready.

"Smell that!" Chet said, as the delicious aroma of the roasting meat reached him. "It must be true that we're going to have a feast. Boy, I can't wait!"

The native band started playing as the boys looked round, smiling. To the cheers of the Indians, the visitors were escorted to a low, decorated table in the public square.

Young Indian girls passed huge dishes of fruits, maize, beans, and meat.

During the meal Tecum-Uman told the boys that he had already sent word to the Guatemalan president requesting that each boy be given a gold souvenir from the buried palace as a token of the country's gratefulness to them.

"We don't expect a reward," said Joe. "We've had a grand time visiting your beautiful country. I wish that everyone in the States could come down here to see it." The old chief looked pleased.

The boys remained in the village for the next two days. Finally federal officers arrived to take the prisoners away. And with them, bearing a large white envelope with an elaborate seal, was a grinning Jorge Almeida.

Jorge hopped off the mule he was riding, with the same adeptness that he had driven his taxi round the mountain curves. "You heroes, *amigos*!" he cried. "Why you not tell me you look for this treasure? Never would I go back to the city!"

After explaining why secrecy had been important,

Tony asked how Jorge had learned about the treasure.

"Why all the papers tell about the great thing you have did," the man said enthusiastically.

Then Jorge told how he had personally called on the president and related his part in the adventure. When he had requested permission that he might be able to come out and see the treasure, the president had said that he could accompany the police and deliver the letter he now carried.

"It is for all of you," he said importantly, handing the envelope to Joe. The letter, signed with the president's name, thanked the boys for the discovery and requested that they each take home a small souvenir from the palace.

Later that afternoon, the four boys and Jorge journeyed out to the ancient site with Tecum-Uman. While the chief led Jorge, highly excited, through the palace rooms, the boys decided on what souvenirs they would choose.

Chet picked up a large, jewelled bowl. "This must be what the king used for his special dinners," he said. "It's just the thing for me!"

A delicately carved bracelet of gold was Frank's choice. He knew Mrs Hardy would like it. And Joe could not resist a small golden idol as a gift for Aunt Gertrude. "It may even try to talk back to her!" He laughed.

As Tony selected an ancient, gold-encrusted bow and arrow, he said, "We mustn't forget Willie Wortman. Those medallions have served their purpose, so I'll give him the one I have. The curse is broken!"

For a short time the Hardys were to be free of a mystery. Then another, called *What Happened at Midnight* was to come their way and involve the brothers in a series of harrowing experiences. But at the moment this was far from their thoughts.

Just then, their cheerful friend Jorge walked in with Tecum-Uman. "This palace hokay!" he exclaimed. His eyes sparkling, he added, "But you must see my new taxi! The horn she is like music. And," he concluded, "brakes very good. I park her back at trading village. We pick her up and you ride to city with me?"

"Sure. But how about that volcano?" Joe asked.

Jorge grinned. "I find new way."